MIDNIGHT RIDE

❧ *A* GATES *Family Mystery* ❧

By Catherine Hapka

Based on characters created for the theatrical

motion picture "National Treasure"

Screenplay by Jim Kouf and Cormac Wibberley & Marianne Wibberley

Story by Jim Kouf and Oren Aviv & Charles Segars

DISNEP PRESS

New York

An Imprint of Disney Book Group

Thank you to those who started this hunt:
Oren Aviv, Charles Segars, and Jim Kouf

🚲 🚲

And those who carry it on:
Christine Cadena, Jason Reed, Rich Thomas,
and Elizabeth Rudnick

MIDNIGHT RIDE

✎ *A* GATES *Family Mystery* ✎

Copyright © 2008 Disney Enterprises, Inc.

All rights reserved. Published by Disney Press, an imprint of Disney Book Group.
No part of this book may be reproduced or transmitted in any form or by
any means, electronic or mechanical, including photocopying, recording, or by any
information storage and retrieval system, without written permission from the
publisher. For information address Disney Press, 114 Fifth Avenue,
New York, New York 10011-5690.

Printed in the United States of America

First Edition
1 3 5 7 9 10 8 6 4 2

Library of Congress Catalog Card Number: 2007906286
ISBN-13: 978-1-4231-0815-3
ISBN-10: 1-4231-0815-9

Map Courtesy of The Library of Congress, Maps and Geography Division

This book is set in 13-point Centaur MT

Visit disneybooks.com

December 16, 1773
Boston

"Whoa, girl! Settle down. One might think you'd never seen Boston town before!" John Raleigh Gates laughed as the mare he was riding spooked at a drove of hogs being herded down the gangplank of a brigantine moored at Griffin's Wharf.

John's father, Thomas, referred to this particular horse only as "the fast bay mare," but John had given her the name Liberty in honor of her independent temperament. Lean of build and sinewy of muscle, she wasn't the largest horse in the stable—John had just turned sixteen years old, but he was tall for his age and broad-shouldered, and his feet hung well below her sides.

Liberty also wasn't the easiest to ride, being prone to fits of bucking when she felt ill-used. But she certainly had to be numbered among the fastest horses John had known and was easily his favorite out of the small livery he operated with his father in their hometown of Concord. He chose her often when he was hired to ride the post or deliver messages, knowing she would carry him where he needed to go in good time.

Now, as she stared wide-eyed at the squealing hogs, her dancing hooves raising dust from the cobblestones, John soothed her with a pat. Even after she started to quiet, his hand lingered, smoothing out the mane—as black and thick as his own hair—that fell down over her withers. His mind wandered back over all the rides they'd had together, all the times she'd shown her heart and loyalty. She was a special horse indeed and not easily replaced. . . .

He shook his head, reminding himself that there would be no need for that sort of melancholy thought if today's errand were successful.

Liberty settled quickly once the hogs waddled their way out of sight behind some barrels, and John pushed her on automatically, dodging a stack of wooden crates in their path and glancing curiously out into the channel as they passed along the crowded docks. He had heard much talk lately of the three tall British ships anchored off Griffin's Wharf—the *Dartmouth*, the *Eleanor*, and the *Beaver*—and was curious to now see them for himself. They were bobbing quietly against their moorings, looking like every other ship in the harbor, apart from the British warships that stood sentinel over them.

"All still here, then," John murmured, more to himself than to the mare. He recalled many discussions over the past month, and comments made by his friend Duncan Winslow, some passing post riders, and various others in Concord, involving all the trouble with the tea ships in Boston. From what he had gathered, the *Dartmouth* had arrived a month earlier loaded with tea from the East India Company, but had not been permitted to unload due to complicated and, in John's estimation, rather dull reasons of taxation. The other two ships had followed later, with the same result.

"It was the Sons of Liberty that stopped the ships from unloading," Duncan had said, his blue eyes bright in his thin, sallow face. "They say last year's Tea Act is like that abominable and ridiculous Stamp Act from when we were children—a craven attempt by the Crown to stunt the freedom of these colonies. That is why the Tea Act so boldly allows the East India Company to import their product duty-free, while our local merchants still must struggle under the

Crown's taxes. It is no wonder so many colonists these days are boycotting tea altogether. And mark my words, the Sons of Liberty will not back down, nor should they!"

John had only the vaguest notion of who the Sons of Liberty were—some sort of political group led, as best he could tell from the gossip, by the well-known political writer Samuel Adams and a Boston merchant named Hancock—and he had even less interest. He paid scant attention to politics, being far more interested in horses and harnesses, or perhaps a rousing game of cricket or ninepins, than in the constant bickering between colonists and Crown, which had been going on as long as he'd been alive. By contrast, Duncan had great interest in such things, and though his fancies were sometimes obscure, John always respected his friend's intelligence and opinions. If Duncan thought this squabble over tea worthy of attention, John didn't doubt that it was.

Even so, his mind didn't linger long on such matters of taxation and politics. There were more important things to worry about this chilly December day. He checked the address he'd brought with him, then touched the pouch at his waist, feeling a bitter pang of guilt. His father and all but one of his sisters thought he was in Boston today to deliver a message to a wealthy tradesman. Only John's next-eldest sister, Alice, knew his true errand; she was his confidante within the family and could always be trusted to advise him honestly.

Squinting up toward the sun, John gauged the hour to be close to half past two. The daylight faded quickly this time of the year, and ice on the roads had kept his pace slow on the way to Boston. As expected, he would have to stay the night with his cousins, who lived over on King Street near the Town House, before riding home to Concord the next day. In the meantime, there was no sense in delaying the inevitable, and so he turned away from the wharf and set forth in search of Dock-Square. Happily it was little trouble to locate it, and once he arrived there he soon spied the silversmith's shop he sought on a cozy block crowded with comfortable frame houses and brick shops. A cat stared at him curiously as he dismounted, then slunk off to hide beneath a landau parked farther down the street.

John tied his horse, shook the long ride out of his legs, grabbed his saddlebags, and entered the shop. Stepping from the bright daylight into its dim, lamplit interior, the half dozen or more men within appeared little more than shadows to his sun-blinded gaze. Even so, he saw them all instantly stop whatever they were doing and turn to stare at him upon his entrance.

One shadowy man separated himself from the rest and hurried over. Now that John's eyes were adjusting, he saw a powerfully built, well-dressed, ruddy-faced man of about forty with intelligent brown eyes and a reddish tinted wig. His brow was creased in an anxious furrow.

"Do you bring news from Faneuil Hall?" the man asked John sharply.

John glanced around, confused. The other men were all still gazing at him curiously, though a group of the younger men had quickly returned to their work at the anvils and trestle tables.

"I beg your pardon, sir?" John said, wondering if the man had mistaken him for someone else. "Er, my name is John Gates. I came from Concord in hopes of showing the owner of this shop some small items I have to sell."

The man sighed and rubbed his face, casting a rather impatient glance toward the front door. "I see. My mistake, then, my lad." He smiled, though it seemed a bit forced.

"My name is Paul Revere. I am the proprietor of this shop. It is a rather busy day and I am short of time, but since you are here let us see what you have brought."

John took a deep breath, trying not to imagine how his father might react if he knew what he was doing. "Thank you, Mr. Revere, sir," he said. "I do not know if these things are of much value. But I am hoping . . ."

He dumped the contents of the saddlebags onto a table nearby. Mr. Revere leaned over for a closer look, sifting through the muddle of metal buckles, spoons, and snuff-boxes with one hand. Next to the fine silverwork for sale in the shop, it looked rather shabby.

John held his breath, thinking of Liberty standing tied outside this very moment. Her future depended on what the silversmith said next. . . .

"Hmm." Revere straightened and glanced at John. "I'm afraid I can't give you much for this lot." He named a sum, one many times smaller than John had hoped.

Bitter disappointment burned through John's body. That was that, then. It seemed that this trip was for naught. He wouldn't be able to save Liberty from being sold to the hateful Mr. Sims after all.

Despite the longstanding enmity between the Sims and Gates families, John had to admit that the elder Sims had a good eye for a horse. There would be no dissuading him from wanting Liberty—nor Thomas Gates from finally giving in and selling her for the offered price. There were simply too many bills to be covered by the meager income from the family's livery and harness-making business.

"But wait a moment." Mr. Revere had started to sweep John's modest collection across the table with his arm, and in the process, tipped open a small, battered snuffbox. He picked something up and held it to the light. "What's this?"

John looked closer as well. "Oh!" he cried in surprise. "I did not know that was in there."

He had recognized the item immediately. It was an old family heirloom, a ring passed down through generations, supposedly from the first Gates to arrive in the New World—Samuel Thomas Gates of Jamestown, Virginia, after whom John's own father was named.

"I'm sorry," he told Revere. "I didn't mean to include that. I'm certain it isn't worth much to anyone outside my family."

"On the contrary." Revere glanced at a few other men who were still watching from the corner of the shop. "This appears to be a very early Mason's ring. Is your father a Freemason, son?"

John shook his head. He'd heard of the Freemasons, a gentlemen's society that claimed many influential Bostonians among its membership, but knew little about the group. He did not think his father had much knowledge of the Freemasons, either.

"Come have a look, Hancock," Revere called, suddenly sounding almost cheerful in contrast to his earlier mood. "What do you think—could this be the omen of good luck that we need this day?"

A long-nosed man of keen expression who appeared to be near Revere's age hurried over to examine the ring. John Gates stared at him. Hancock—could this possibly be *the* John Hancock of whom Duncan had spoken so many times in connection with the Sons of Liberty?

"Aye, my friend," Hancock said to Revere. "An omen indeed."

"Agreed. I hope our new friend will include it in his offerings. If so, I think we can extend him a much better deal." Revere named a sum—one so high that for a moment John thought he was joking.

But Revere repeated the offer, already reaching for a purse lying nearby. John gulped, realizing that the silversmith was indeed serious. He wanted to pay John a small fortune—well over what he would need to convince his father not to sell Liberty. But at what price? John was confident and audacious by nature, and there was little that he feared in the mortal world. The one exception was his father's temper. If Thomas discovered that the heirloom ring was gone . . .

But then thinking of Liberty, awaiting him faithfully just outside, John nodded quickly. Some matters were worth nearly any risk.

"I accept your generous offer with gratitude, sir," he told Revere.

"Good." Revere smiled at him and counted out the price. "Then the deal is done."

Meanwhile, Hancock had stepped forward to peer out the shop door. "It is nearing three o'clock," he said urgently. "We should go."

Revere nodded, tucking the Mason's ring away in his waistcoat. "Are you coming to the meeting, son?" he asked John, by now sounding downright jovial.

"Meeting, sir?" John repeated.

The other men from the shop were now hurrying forward to join Hancock and Revere. "Don't tell me you haven't heard, mate?" one of the younger silversmiths exclaimed. "Why, no one in Boston has thought of anything else since we adjourned the town meeting earlier today!"

Seeing John's confusion, Revere clapped him on the back and smiled. "Come along with us, young Mr. Gates," he urged. "All shall become clear."

Never one to turn down a possible adventure, John shrugged and agreed. He did, after all, have quite a deal of time to kill in Boston. Revere quickly helped John stow Liberty safely in a nearby stable, and then they took off on foot.

What followed next later seemed to John a kind of dream, more like a rousing tale heard at night at his brother-in-law's tavern than something actually experienced. He went with Revere and the others to the Old South Meeting House. Upon entering he stifled a gasp as he noticed that the room was full of not only angry colonists but Indians as well. Catching his look, Revere sent John a reassuring glance. A moment later, John realized that these were not Indians at all, but rather colonists disguised as Natives. Relieved he moved further inside.

The air was ripe with shouts, nervous laughter, and the odors of too many people too closely situated. Despite the chill outside, inside it was warm to the point of stuffiness. Swept up in it all, John listened for the next several hours, as a succession of men climbed to the front of the assembly to make eloquent and often fiery speeches.

At first John was disappointed to realize that the meeting focused only on the continuing dispute over unloading the British tea from the ships he'd noted at Griffin's Wharf.

But as John continued to listen, he put together what he was hearing from these passionate men with what he already knew from the comments of Duncan and others. Before long his own passion had climbed until it reached a fever pitch. Why, indeed, should the colonists suffer the tea to be landed under such unfair conditions? He had never truly thought it through before. The Tea Act wasn't just another boring act of taxation from Parliament. It was clearly nothing but an attempt to bring the colonies to heel and destroy any hopes of self-reliance! The solution was simple—

if the tea was never delivered, it would surely teach the Crown a lesson about trying to squelch the colonies' freedoms.

Just after a man named Quincy had finished speaking, another man entered to announce that Governor Hutchinson had denied their demand to send the ships back to England without unloading their cargo. A ripple of outrage began to travel through the crowd, until a weary but distinguished-looking older man of leonine mien stood up.

"That is the great Patriot leader, Mr. Samuel Adams, my boy," Revere murmured to John. The silversmith had kept John close to his side throughout the meeting, often explaining things when John looked confused. "What you are witnessing now is the culmination of many months of planning to protest the Tea Act," Revere added.

Adams's words were brief and his tone harsh. "This meeting can do nothing more to save the country," he announced in a loud, rallying voice.

"Boston Harbor, a teapot tonight!" someone shouted hoarsely from the gallery. "Hurrah for Griffin's Wharf!"

More shouts arose from all around the meeting hall, and John found himself caught up in the excitement, joining in with full voice. Someone standing near him let out a war whoop, which was echoed across the room. After that, it seemed the most natural thing in the world that the entire group should pour out into the cold, moonlit streets and hurry to the wharf a few blocks away. In this excitement John lost track of Revere, Hancock, and the others, but it seemed not to matter—all members of the group were now his friends. A burly man who appeared to be a longshore-man grabbed him as he neared the dock.

"You look like a strong Patriot, lad," the longshoreman said. "Come with me."

John nodded and followed willingly. While many watched quietly from shore, John found himself aboard the *Dartmouth.* He quickly did as directed, hauling heavy tea chests up from the hold and dumping their contents into the still waters below. Before long his muscles ached, and he was bruised from the strenuous work, but still he con-tinued on with his new compatriots, swept away by the clear righteousness of the undertaking. . . .

He had no idea what hour it was by the time the task was finished, the group dispersed, and he made his way back to Dock-Square to collect his horse. Everything had happened so fast that he was having trouble taking it in properly, but he couldn't shake the feeling that something important had just taken place. Important for the colonies, and important for him, John Raleigh Gates. He fell asleep on his cousin's floor exhausted but strangely exhilarated. His life had taken a new direction—he was sure of it.

Charles River

Ferry to Charles-Town
is about half Mile over

Mill Pond

B: N: Mill Dam.

HARBOUR

Fort Hill

S. Battery.

Old Wharfe

Old Wharfe

Old Wharfe

One

"Aye, but it's a hot one today," John commented, pushing through the door into the kitchen.

His sister Alice looked up from the table, where she was breaking eggs into a bowl. "How is the colt looking this morning?" she inquired, her pretty, heart-shaped face tinted pink from the heat in the steamy room.

"Better. I expect he'll pull through again after all." John collapsed onto a wooden chair, as far from the fire as it was possible to get, and mopped his brow. He and his father had bred only one mare that year, and her foal had not had any easy time of it, being born during a late-season snowstorm and winding up rather weak and sickly. But John's careful nursing had helped the baby pull through that first crisis and several more, and just now, in late July, it was finally beginning to seem healthy more often than not.

John's second-eldest sister, Elizabeth, bustled in at the moment, a freshly plucked cockerel swinging from her good hand. Elizabeth, like eldest sister Mary and third-eldest Sarah, had the red hair and hazel eyes of their mother, who had died of consumption when Sarah was a baby. Alice, John, and thirteen-year-old twins Mercy and Humility had been born of their father's second wife, Constance, who had died in childbirth delivering the twins. After that, Thomas had never remarried.

"Ready for some breakfast, John?" Elizabeth asked cheerfully, pushing aside the dog that had followed her in and was now sniffing hopefully at the dead bird. Elizabeth was always cheerful, even though some might say she had little reason to be, considering she'd had one of her hands so badly burned as a baby that it was all but useless now, and also that at age twenty-four she had never married. Still, she seemed not to mind her lot in life, caring devotedly for her father and the siblings still at home, and doting over Mary and Sarah's young children as if they were her own. She had even overcome her lifelong fear of horses so that she could occasionally ride to visit Sarah, who now lived with her family in the neighboring village of Sudbury.

"I'm ready," John said. "Where is Father? I have not yet seen him this morning in the stable."

That was no surprise, really. Over the last several years, Thomas Gates had allowed more and more of the business of running the livery and harness shop to fall to his only son. John was even-tempered, quick of wit, and very good at remembering even the most mundane details of his neighbors' lives. This made him much more popular with customers than the rather dreamy—and often gruff— Thomas. Not only that, but John seemed to have a magic touch with horses. Even the more difficult animals seemed to feel as kindly toward him as he did toward every one of them. It had been thus since John was old enough to toddle out to the stable at his father's heel.

Before Elizabeth or Alice could answer John's question, Thomas strode into the kitchen, followed by the twins, who were laughing over some secret of their own, as usual. "Morning, son," Thomas greeted John with a nod. His brown hair was normally several shades lighter than John's, but today it was so dark with sweat that it was difficult to tell. "Things all right outside?"

"Fine. Looks like the foal is better again—I think it may be for good this time."

Thomas shook his head. "And to think I was ready to

give up on that one. I suppose I should have believed you when you said he'd pull through." He let out a brief, wondering laugh. "My own father would have said you've inherited the family gift of horsemanship. According to him, it traces all the way back to my namesake Samuel Thomas Gates's wife, Elizabeth, who was said to be a better horseman than any man in Jamestown."

John smiled to hide a flash of guilt at the mention of their ancestors, which only served to remind him of the ring he'd sold to Mr. Revere back in December. Even now, some seven months later, Thomas hadn't noticed its absence, but John often wondered what would happen if he did.

Regardless, he couldn't quite regret what he'd done. For one thing, the sale of the ring had saved Liberty from being sold, just as he'd hoped. John had claimed the money came from a wealthy post customer grateful for his speedy service, though his father hadn't asked too many questions after seeing the amount. It had been more than enough to pay off the bills, which, as John had expected, meant Thomas no longer saw any reason to sell his best horse to his worst enemy.

But that wasn't all. That fateful day in December had

also led John to a continuing contact with Mr. Revere and his friends, which he was finding doubly rewarding. Their friendship had brought John into the world of the Patriots, colonists who wished openly for independence from British rule, and John now counted himself strongly among their number. In addition, his new Patriot friends had brought him much more work as a post rider, delivering messages and mail throughout Massachusetts and the surrounding colonies.

That extra work meant more income for John's family, which badly needed it. His father had never been particularly clever with money—he had always depended on a wife to help manage that sort of thing. Although Elizabeth was a great help in household matters, she had no interest in, or talent for, numbers, leaving that, too, to John.

Thomas took a seat at the table, stretching out his legs, which were even leaner and longer than John's own. "What have you to do today, son?" he asked.

"I've been hired to carry some letters over to Lexington," John replied, smiling his thanks to Alice as she set a mug before him on the table. "Liberty was hired by a post rider out of Salem yesterday, so I'll have to ride the red gelding today. Even so, it shouldn't take me long." He paused to take a drink, then glanced over the top of his mug at his father. "If you have time today, Father, that big gray horse that was here last week kicked out some boards in the stalls, and I haven't had a chance yet to mend them."

"Perhaps." Thomas's voice held a faraway note.

John sighed, knowing what that tone meant. The broken boards would still be waiting when he returned from his ride. By now, he knew better than to press the point.

Finishing his breakfast, John pushed back from the table. "I'd best be off," he said. "I should return easily within the day if all goes well."

"Let me walk out with you, John." Alice stepped toward him with a smile. "I need to fetch more water from the well."

Elizabeth turned away from the fire, raising her bad hand in farewell even as she kept stirring a cooking pot with the good one. "Safe ride today, brother," she called. "I'll have your favorite boiled pudding for you on your return."

The twins added their good-byes, but Thomas barely looked up from his food. "Safe ride, son."

John and Alice exited the house, walking out through the small kitchen garden that filled the space between the house and the outbuildings that lay out back. John had always loved the Gates family home, which had been built by his great-grandfather, John Patrick Gates, upon arriving in Massachusetts from the south, and passed down through the generations since. It had begun as a modest saltbox and grown into a proper Georgian hall-and-parlor house over the years, its clapboard siding weathered to a soft gray. Behind lay not only the springhouse and privy, but also the good-size stable and its connected workshop, where Thomas made repairs on tack and other leather goods, and sometimes made and sold new harness as well.

After arriving in Massachusetts, John Patrick Gates and his son had quickly become known in their new home for some of the finest leatherwork in the northern colonies. However, Thomas had never quite managed to match their skill, and John had only basic competence in the craft, being far more interested in the creatures that wore it than in the tack and harness itself. Still, they remained known as the best place in the area for harness repair, especially since John's friend Duncan, who was clever with his hands, had recently taken over some of the finer work. If only Thomas would step up . . .

"Don't be hard on Father, John," Alice said, breaking into his thoughts.

John glanced at her, surprised as ever by the way she seemed to know what he was thinking. "I am less hard on him than he is on himself," he said. "Do not blame his bitterness and lack of ambition on me!"

"Of course I am doing no such thing." Alice sighed. "However, it must be difficult for Father to accept that you are losing interest in treasure hunting. It used to bond you together so."

"I doubt he has even noticed that I have outgrown the family obsession." John grimaced. "As long as the mystery of that blasted medallion remains unsolved, I suspect he'll not take notice of much else."

Like the tradition of horsemanship in their family, an interest in treasure hunting had been passed down through the generations. That interest, too, had begun in the time of Samuel Thomas Gates, who was said to have discovered some trove of native treasures soon after arriving in Jamestown.

In the generations since, some had seen it as little more than a hobby. But for others—Thomas foremost among them—it had become an obsession, focused mostly around an ancient wooden medallion. Family legend had it that the medallion had been given to Samuel Thomas Gates by an old native woman who claimed it held the key to great riches.

John sighed as he recalled many hours spent examining that medallion as well as reading old letters, poring over maps, and tramping across hill and dale in search of treasure. What Alice said was true—father and son *had* enjoyed a special bond in those days. As the only boy in the family, John had been the recipient of all the old family lore. And for a while he had enjoyed it, especially on those occasions when he and Thomas actually managed to unearth some modest treasure—a box of old gold coins long since buried and forgotten, a few bits of silver flatware hidden in an abandoned fireplace. Still, as a child, John had always been most intrigued by the rumors of the Lost City of Gold and other vast, unimaginable treasures. After a while, tracking down the origin of a dusty old medallion or finding a few tarnished spoons began to seem far less exciting, though Thomas was always quick to admonish him for such opinions.

"It's all about the details, my boy," he'd said on many

occasions. "A true treasure hunter sees not only the larger picture, but also the importance of each step of the search."

"At least that's one useful thing I learned from Father," John muttered to himself now as he walked beside Alice.

"What was that?" Alice asked.

"Never mind."

They reached the family's well, which stood a few yards outside the main stable doors. Alice stopped beside it, gazing at John with concern in her blue eyes, which so well matched his own.

"In any case, it is a shame you two have grown apart recently," she said. "I think Father misses you."

John shrugged, avoiding her steady gaze. "I cannot help that. If he would only spend more time in the stable and harness shop rather than brooding over that medallion or wandering off on his treasure hunts, he would have little need to miss me at all. I'm quite certain our family finances would be the better for it as well."

"Perhaps." For a moment Alice looked as if she wanted to say more. Then she turned toward the well. "Safe ride, John."

John did his best to put the whole subject out of mind

as he entered the dusty, leather-scented stable. But even as he tacked up the stocky, thick-necked liver chestnut he planned to ride on the first leg of that day's journey, he couldn't seem to shake the wistful mood that nearly always settled over him when he thought too much about his father. It wasn't until he'd swung a leg over the chestnut and felt the animal's muscles tense with anticipation of the ride that he was able to regain his usual temper.

"Come along, Big Red," he said, double-checking the saddlebags to make sure the packet of letters was inside and then urging the horse out toward the road. "It is time for a ride."

As predicted, John was back in Concord well before sunset. He'd traded the chestnut gelding for a skinny and rather jumpy bay at a Lexington livery, and had found the new mount quite diverting on the ride back as he entertained himself trying to guess what the creature would spook at next.

By the time he crossed the Old North Bridge, he had grown weary of the game and began to miss faithful Liberty, who was at least a bit more discerning in her anxieties. He forgot all that, though, as he spotted two familiar figures fishing off the bank of the river nearby.

The pair spotted him at the same time. "Look out, Duncan," one of them exclaimed. "It's John Gates, the distinguished post rider, back from carrying important letters for the rich and successful."

John grinned and dismounted, hurrying with horse in tow toward his two best friends. George Chase and Duncan Winslow couldn't have been more different from each other. George was an inch or two shorter than John but nearly twice as broad, with a beefy, good-natured face beneath an unruly shock of fair hair. He was good with his fists but slow to anger and the most loyal friend imaginable—John had known him since before birth, as their mothers had been close friends.

Duncan was a couple of years older than John and George, but much smaller and weaker. He had been born with one leg twisted and stunted, and walked with the aid of a cane. However, his mind was bright and alert, his eyesight was outstanding, and he was clever and nimble with his long, slender hands.

"What have you two been doing while I was out there

earning a living?" John asked the pair jokingly. "Lazing about, I expect?"

George chuckled but Duncan ignored the joke. He dropped his fishing pole and climbed to his feet with the aid of his cane, peering up into John's face with his intense, long-lashed, dark eyes.

"We were just discussing the latest news brought by a post rider who stopped to change horses at your stable this noon," he said. "Have you heard?"

When John shook his head, George explained, "Some bigwigs down in Virginia colony have drafted a statement in response to the unfairness of the Intolerable Acts."

"Bigwigs indeed—it is the well-known Patriot politician, Colonel Washington, who is leading this struggle." As he spoke, Duncan tapped out a staccato rhythm with his cane against a rock on the riverbank. "And the famous orator Patrick Henry and a planter and politician named Mason with him. They intend to convene a sort of continental congress to decide how the colonies should react to the recent outrages."

"Indeed? It is about time someone did something to show the Crown we won't be cowed by such tactics." John's fists automatically clenched around the reins as he thought of the series of strict laws passed over the past few months. Collectively, these laws were known by many colonists as the Intolerable or Coercive Acts and they involved everything from the closure of the port in Boston to the running of the government of Massachusetts to the rules over the quartering of the king's soldiers on private property.

George grinned. "Perhaps you'd better offer your services to Mr. Washington then, Gates. Aren't you our own local activist?"

John's momentary outrage passed, and he grinned back. Naturally, he had told his friends of his participation in what had since become known throughout the colonies as the Destruction of the Tea, though he'd sworn them to secrecy. He planned to tell no one else, aside from Alice, of his adventures that cold December evening.

Duncan's eyes were still glittering with excitement. "This is important," he said. "It shows that we in Massachusetts Bay Colony have the other colonies as allies against British oppression! After all, most of the Intolerable Acts are clearly aimed straight at us here in Massachusetts as punishment for the adventures of John and his friends in Boston Harbor that night last winter."

"That much is true." John shook his head, anger bubbling up anew as he pondered the injustice of the various Intolerable Acts. "They do not even hide it in the case of the Boston Port Act, which punishes all by closing the port, including those who were not in any way involved in the Destruction of the Tea. That is completely unfair! And then the outrageous Government Act—"

George shrugged. "Let us not get too excited over this," he broke in, his voice as measured as ever. "Perhaps these Acts will all be repealed again in the end, as with the Stamp Act back when we were boys. I'm certain the Crown has no wish to pick a fight with the colonies, nor we with them."

John wasn't surprised by his friend's words; George had never had much interest in larger matters of politics and world affairs. And up until last December, John had felt the same. Why waste the energy on something that seemed so distant from his everyday life? The phrase "no taxation without representation" had always seemed little more than a slogan that caused many adults to mutter and scowl but held little meaning in his own life.

However, his opinions had changed after that night and now lined up more closely with Duncan's. He now saw the importance of staying apprised of current events, no matter how distant they seemed. After all, if the colonists did not object when England overstepped her bounds, what was to stop the king from doing worse in the future? He was about to open his mouth and express some of this when the skinny bay horse, which had been grazing on the riverbank at the end of its reins, suddenly snorted and lifted its head in alarm.

"You boys!" a voice shouted a second later. "What are you doing there? Up to no good, are we?"

John winced as he recognized the voice. He turned to see a portly, florid-faced man hurrying toward them.

"Speaking of intolerable," he whispered to Duncan, "here's Mr. Sims!"

George was already grabbing his fishing pole along with Duncan's. "Never mind," he called to Mr. Sims in his most ingratiating tone. "We were just moving on."

Two

"Are you sure you wouldn't like to take a horse?" John asked Alice. "Your spinning wheel is heavy for you to carry all that way."

Alice laughed, hoisting the wheel in both arms. "All that way? Do not be silly, brother," she said. "It is only a ten-minute walk to the inn. I should hate to trouble a horse for that!"

"At least let me walk you there." Not allowing any more argument, John took the wheel from her and tucked it under his arm. "It would be nice to say hello to Mary and Oliver anyway—I haven't seen them all week."

"All right, then. I would enjoy the company. Thank you."

Brother and sister set off down the hard-packed, dusty dirt road in the direction of the village's public house, which was operated by their eldest sister, Mary, and her husband, Oliver Miller. Alice was planning to spend the morning there spinning and gossiping with Mary, as they often did when both had enough free time. Elizabeth had been invited as well, though she had chosen to remain at home to take care of the washing.

"Do you realize Mary and Oliver will have been wed ten years this autumn?" Alice commented as they walked.

John glanced at her, impressed as always by the way she kept so many facts in her head. She was perhaps even better at remembering the minutiae of everyday life than he was.

"I had forgotten," he admitted. "Then again, I was quite young when it happened."

"True enough." Alice grimaced, glancing at the house they were passing at the moment, which was inhabited by the Sims family. "Too bad Mr. Sims can't seem to forget."

John nodded. Back when he was only six years old and Mary a fresh-faced girl of sixteen, one of the Sims sons had wished to court the eldest Gates daughter. However, Mary had preferred Oliver Miller, and he had returned her interest. Sims and his son had never forgiven the perceived snub, and relations between the two families had remained tense ever since.

Alice shook her head as they moved on past the Sims

house toward the center of the village, a cluster of tidy frame buildings dominated by the tall, shingled spire of the church. "Considering the uncertain political climate these days, it seems the least we could do is remain on good terms with our own neighbors."

"I agree," John said. "It's all a bit ridiculous. But after nearly ten years of enmity, I doubt anything will change. Especially with two such stubborn fools involved."

Alice glanced at him. "You mean Father and Mr. Sims?"

"Who else?" John laughed. However, talking of Sims—and the political mood of the day—reminded him of the riverside conversation he had had with George and Duncan almost a month earlier. Since that time, George's prediction that things would settle down again had proven decidedly *not* true. If anything, tensions between the colonies and England were only growing worse, though aside from a shortage of a few necessary goods caused by the closing of the port, it hadn't affected John's daily life much.

After dropping Alice off at the tavern and trading a quick hello with his relatives, John hurried home. He had no messages to deliver that day, so after a quick check on the horses, he headed into the harness shop to see if his father needed him for anything. There he found a pile of harness waiting to be mended—but no sign of Thomas.

John sighed, recalling that his father had seemed particularly distracted at breakfast that day. That, in combination with his absence now, could mean only one thing. Thomas must be off on yet another fool's mission involving that old medallion or some other wild-goose chase.

"I suppose it's up to me, again, then," John muttered. With a sigh, he sat down in front of the pile of leather and set to work.

He was still at it some two hours later when he heard the clatter of hooves in the courtyard outside. Dropping the breast collar he was stitching, he headed out just in time to see a rider swing to the ground in front of the stable.

"Good day, sir," John said politely, hurrying forward to take the bridle of the rider's sweaty black horse. "Will you have need of—oh! Mr. Revere—a pleasure to see you."

Despite some correspondence by letter, John hadn't seen Revere in more than eight months. However, he would have recognized him anywhere. The silversmith smiled at him.

"Ah, young Mr. Gates," he said, sounding pleased. "I was told I would find you at this livery stable. How have you been since our fine adventure last winter?"

"I am well. But—what are you doing so far from your shop?" John asked.

Revere stomped his feet and stretched his arms over his head, as John himself often did after a long time on the road. "I do not spend all my time bent over spoons and tankards," he said with a chuckle. "Lately I have been doing some work for our fellow Patriots, primarily as a messenger. I am on my way to New York at the moment, bearing some very important news for our allies there."

"I see," John said. "So you require a fresh horse? If you like, you can take my best mare. She is the fastest horse in Concord—possibly in all of Massachusetts Colony."

Revere's black horse was standing at John's side, flanks heaving and nostrils blowing in the hot August sun. Noticing the animal's condition, John led it to the trough nearby and allowed it to drink. But most of his attention remained focused on Revere.

Revere smiled, though his eyes had gone serious. "I am indeed in need of a horse, lad, but you'll want to keep your fast mare for yourself," he said, removing his hat and fanning himself with it. "You are a post rider, are you not?" At

John's nod, he went on. "I am hoping you are available to pick up and deliver a message for me as I cannot do two jobs at once. You would need to ride to Connecticut and find a Mr. Nathan Hale, who teaches at a school there. He will deliver you the message, which you will need to carry to another Patriot back here in Massachusetts—Mr. Hale shall provide you with the second name and address when you reach him. This is a very important message, and it needs to go with someone we can trust. Naturally I thought of my bold young post-riding friend from last December." He winked, then went solemn again. "Does that sound like a job you can handle, my boy? Answer me truly."

"I would be honored, sir," John said with a growing sense of excitement. What had begun as a dull, perfectly ordinary summer day was turning into anything but! "I shall see to your horse, then have Liberty saddled and ready to depart within the hour!"

"Liberty?" Revere repeated curiously. "Hold on—is that what you call your mare?"

John blushed. "I know it is rather silly but . . ."

"Not at all." Revere clapped him on the shoulder. "In fact, hearing that name reassures me all the more that I've chosen a true Patriot for this job. I shall rest easy on the road to New York knowing that John Gates and his Liberty are working for the side of right."

John wasn't entirely sure the older man wasn't mocking him. But even if he was, he didn't mind. It was flattering to think that Mr. Revere had come to him with such an important errand.

"Choose any horse you wish, sir," he called over his shoulder as he hurried the black horse into the stable. "I'll just need to tell my sister I'm off on a delivery. Then I shall help you tack up and be on my way!"

John's excitement had worn off somewhat by the time he reached New London, Connecticut, a couple days later. At times, as he had ridden the dusty, familiar post roads along the way, he'd had to remind himself that this wasn't just another delivery of family letters or business correspondence. It certainly hadn't felt much different most of the time. He had still had to keep a lookout for wild animals and other dangers; still had to stop periodically to let his horse rest and drink; still ended up each day sore of limb and weary of mind. But thinking of the gleam in Mr. Revere's eye when he'd entrusted this mission to him had usually refreshed John quickly and reminded him that this ride was, indeed, of a different sort.

He reached the lively seaport town of New London shortly after dark and spent the night at the local inn. Early the next morning he inquired after Mr. Nathan Hale and was directed to the Union Grammar School just down the road, where Hale was headmaster. John had traded Liberty at a post stable along the way and now rode a phlegmatic dapple gray gelding who seemed more plow horse than road horse but had been the only mount available at John's last stop. Even with the heavy beast's lazy trot and plodding canter, it didn't take long to reach the schoolhouse.

The Union School was housed in a modest, white clapboard building with a squat bell tower set atop a gambrel roof. Several large windows on the side were open to admit the cool morning air.

As the hour was still very early, John wasn't sure the headmaster would be at the school yet. But he'd barely dismounted when he heard peals of laughter from within the building. Surprised by the timbre of the laughter, he hurried forward and peered in through the school's front door. Sure enough, he saw a group of girls inside!

For a moment, John wondered if he had the wrong place after all. One did not often see girls at a Latin school such as this one. But the young man standing at the front of the schoolroom perfectly matched the description Revere had given him. Mr. Nathan Hale was perhaps three years older than John and an inch or two taller, with fair skin, a shock of flaxen hair, and intelligent blue eyes peering out from beneath slightly darker brows. His build was athletic and his mien handsome.

As if sensing him, Hale looked up and saw John. "Good morning," he called. "Can I help you?"

John stepped inside, trying not to feel self-conscious as all the girls immediately turned to stare at him. "Er, Mr. Paul Revere sent me," he said. "I was to pick up a message for delivery."

"Oh, I see!" Hale looked surprised. "Just a moment, young ladies. I shall continue our lesson after I take care of this business."

"Of course, Mr. Hale!" one of the girls sang out, causing the rest to giggle wildly. As Hale walked through the classroom toward John, most of the girls immediately began whispering to one another behind their hands.

When Hale reached the doorway where John stood he glanced out past him, as if expecting someone else. "Mr. Revere could not come himself?" he asked in a low tone.

John shook his head. "He was called to New York," he explained. "But he wished not to delay this errand, and so sent me in his place. My name is John Gates of Concord, Massachusetts. Mr. Revere asked that I show you this." John held out a piece of paper with an odd combination of letters on it. While unreadable to John, Hale seemed reassured by it.

"So he did," Hale said, nodding. Then he began to chuckle, noting that John was staring in confusion at the schoolhouse full of girls. "I imagine you are wondering about my students," he said. "Most people do. I happen to believe that young ladies are equally deserving of secondary education as young men. That is why I open the schoolhouse to them for a couple of hours in the morning before my boys arrive."

"Oh, I—I see." It was too bad Hale's school wasn't closer to Concord, John thought. His sister Alice would have enjoyed greatly the chance to increase her education.

The twins, too, were clever enough to benefit from learning beyond the very basic lessons of dame school.

But John forgot about that as Hale reached into his jacket and pulled out a sealed letter. "This is the message I was to give to Mr. Revere," he told John in a quiet voice clearly not meant to carry to his students' eager ears; most of the girls were still staring in their direction. "I know Mr. Revere would not have sent you in his place if he did not trust you for the job. But please—guard it well, my friend. It is vitally important to our Patriot cause."

"I will." John took the letter. "Where shall I deliver it?"

"The address is there." Hale pointed to a few lines on the outside of the folded paper. "It goes to my old Yale schoolmate Mr. Alden in Springfield, Massachusetts." He peered at John, his startlingly blue eyes seeming to hold a question. "I am sure Mr. Revere has impressed on you the urgency of this matter. We know not when the political situation—" He stopped himself, glancing at the girls. Then he shrugged. "In any case, this message could prove to be very important. Now, do you know the way to Springfield, my friend?"

John nodded. "I have visited Springfield many times," he

assured Hale. "There is a stable there owned by a Mr. Justin Morgan, whose best stallion is the sire of my favorite mare, Liberty."

"You have given the name Liberty to your favorite horse?" Hale chuckled. "Ah, now I see why Mr. Revere has chosen you for this mission! I feel confident that our views are concordant." He extended a hand toward John. "Safe passage, my new friend. And please give Alden my best when you see him—tell him I shall send a more personal letter soon."

It was another few days' ride from New London to Springfield. This time, John arrived late in the afternoon. The horse he was riding at the time was stumbling with exhaustion by then—it had been a long ride from the last post stop, and the August heat was oppressive. Luckily, John knew exactly where to go for a fresh mount. He headed straight for Mr. Morgan's farm, a pleasing homestead of flat, green fields and pastures abutting the Connecticut River.

"John Gates!" Mr. Morgan cried, looking up from fixing a fence board as John rode in. Morgan was a thin, narrow-shouldered man with a face rather long but full of kindness. He was not only a farmer and stallioneer, but also a musical composer and teacher of singing, and even his speaking voice was pleasantly musical in tone. "Is it really you? What brings you to this part of the world? How is your family—and of course that fine bay mare of yours? And the colt?"

"The mare is well, as am I, and the family, too." John swung down from the saddle and led his mount to water. "The new colt had been doing poorly, as we wrote you. But he is much better now."

"Ah, good, good." Morgan shaded his eyes against the sun and smiled at John. "And what is the mood in Concord these days? What talk is there of these Intolerable Acts?"

He and John chatted about politics, farming, and the weather for a few more minutes while Morgan prepared another horse. It was tempting to accept the farmer's offer to stay for supper, but John reluctantly declined. The urgency of his message pressed upon him. After getting directions to Mr. Alden's house, which lay just a few miles away, he said farewell and set off again.

The new horse, a dark bay gelding, was nimble and fit

and carried John quickly to his destination. Alden's house was a small frame building with casement windows, located on the very edge of town and backing up to untamed forest land. John dismounted and walked up to the front door, which stood slightly ajar.

"Hello?" John called uncertainly. "My name is John Gates. I carry a letter for Mr. Alden from Mr. Nathan Hale."

For a moment there was no response from within. Then a weak voice called out, "I am here—please, help me!"

John pushed open the door, a bit confused by the response. But he understood soon enough. Lying on the floor just inside the house was a man. And by the look of the gaping wounds in his chest and the dark stain seeping into the wooden floorboards, he was rapidly bleeding to death!

Three

"What has happened to you?" John cried, hurrying in and dropping to his knees by the man's side. "Are you Mr. Alden?"

"I am." Alden gazed up at him, his voice little more than a feeble croak. "But I shall not be much longer, I fear. Let it be known that it was the regulars who have killed me, only for being a Patriot."

John gulped. He'd long known that the British soldiers, known as regulars, had little patience for Patriot activity. That had been proven clearly enough some four and a half years earlier at what was known among Patriots as the Boston Massacre, when soldiers had fired upon a rioting crowd and killed five colonists. That event had been shocking enough, but this seemed to John even worse—an individual Patriot killed in his own home! It seemed the stuff of story, not reality.

"Let me find something to stop the bleeding," John said. "Then I'll go for help."

"No!" Before John could stand up, Alden stopped him with a hand on his arm. His grip was surprisingly strong. "Please. It is too late for me. But you said you have word from Nathan. Can you tell me what he has sent?"

"Er, not exactly." John felt helpless. What matter was any type of correspondence now? Alden lay dying! "It is—it is a letter involving, er, important Patriot matters, I believe." He cast a nervous glance around the dimly-lit room, half fearing that the regulars who'd shot Alden might still be lurking in the shadows. "It is sealed. All I know is that both Mr. Hale and my friend Mr. Paul Revere of Boston found it urgent that I deliver it here."

"I see." Alden's eyes drifted shut, and for a second John thought he was gone. But then the eyes opened again, bleary but focused on John's face. "And you, messenger. You say you know my friend Nathan, and also Mr. Revere. Are you Patriot as well, then?"

"I am!" John said immediately. Seeing doubt in Alden's fading eyes, he added proudly, "Patriot enough to have taken part in the Destruction of the Tea last December."

"Truly? You were there that night?" Alden blinked, an act which seemed to require most of his remaining strength. "Then perhaps it would be all right . . . yes, it is necessary—you must open this letter that Nathan has sent and take over the mission on behalf of our fellow Patriots."

"What? Me?" John glanced at the letter, which he'd dropped nearby in his haste to reach Alden's side. "Er, I could ride back to Hale, see what he wants to do—"

"There's no time for that!" Alden took in a shallow breath. "If this letter is what I believe it to be, the hunt has begun." His voice was growing so weak now that John had to lean in closer to hear, holding his breath against the mingling scents of blood and gunpowder. Alden continued to speak, every word now clearly causing him considerable struggle. "It cannot fall into the hands of the king's men," he whispered hoarsely. He peered intensely up into John's eyes, as if still trying to see if he could trust him. "Follow the clues. Bring what you find to the attention of other Patriots. It is time to put the heat on the Loyalists." His eyes fluttered shut.

"Mr. Alden?" John said uncertainly.

But there was no answer. Alden was dead.

For a moment John continued to kneel there, staring down at the man's body. Eventually, not knowing what else to do, he stood and walked over to retrieve the letter from where he had dropped it on the floor.

He turned it over in his hands a few times. From that night in Boston Harbor up until a few minutes ago, playing at being a Patriot activist had seemed mostly just fun. Now he was starting to realize that it was no game after all. Did he dare involve himself further?

He took a deep breath, deciding he had no choice. He opened Hale's letter, finding it to be a single sheet of paper. On it was printed a familiar image, one that John recognized immediately, for he had seen it many times before over his lifetime—a drawing of a serpent whose body had been cut into eight pieces, with the initials of the various colonies beside each piece and the words *Join, or Die* printed beneath the entire picture. It was a political cartoon by Mr. Benjamin Franklin of Philadelphia, one that dated back to a few years before John was born in the time leading up to the French and Indian War.

Stepping to the doorway where the light was better, he saw a few words scribbled beneath the image:

Word from S. A. The time seems close at hand. Follow this to the treasure we shall require for liberty to triumph.

John read the words over several times. As far as he could see, there was nothing else on the paper aside from the cartoon and Mr. Alden's name and address. But what could those brief lines mean? Alden's dying words had seemed to indicate that he expected the letter to contain some kind of clue—and the word "treasure" implied the same. Was the cartoon meant to be a clue? If it was, John had no idea how to interpret it.

For a moment he considered going against Alden's wishes and returning to Hale's school. After all, he must have written the note—he could give it to someone else who might have a greater use for it . . .

But that idea passed as quickly as it had come. John had already been away from home nearly a week. Another long journey south into Connecticut wasn't practical. And Alden had been insistent . . . John would just have to hope that he figured out the message in due time. If not, he could decide later what to do.

Pocketing the letter, he headed outside, carefully avoiding sight of the still figure on the floor. It was growing late. He would ride back to Mr. Morgan's, ask his help in reporting the discovery of Alden's body to the local authorities, and then ride for home first thing in the morning.

"And so he told me to follow the clues in the letter to put the heat on the Tories," John said. "A moment later he breathed his last."

"Wow!" Duncan's eyes shone with excitement in the flickering light of the candle on the table. He glanced from John's face to the Franklin cartoon spread on the table between them and then back again. "So this is supposed to hold the clue?"

John leaned back in his seat. He and his two best friends were sitting in Mary and Oliver's tavern. After arriving home from Springfield two nights earlier, John had been too busy seeing to horses, harness, and stable to tell his friends about his adventure. But now it was evening, the chores were caught up at last, and he was filling them in. A part of him hoped their fresh eyes would bring clearer meaning to the mysterious letter.

George, who was sitting beside Duncan, shot an uneasy glance toward a rather raucous group seated across the room. "Keep your voice down, Duncan," he murmured. "Everyone knows that lot over there is loyal to the Crown."

"Indeed." Duncan shot the other group a dirty look, though none of its member were presently glancing in his direction. "Rotten Tories . . ."

John looked over at the other group, too. Among its number he recognized several of his neighbors, including Mr. Wright, the village's most successful cobbler. George was correct—Wright was well known around town as a staunch Loyalist, as quick to defend the king's dominion over the colonies as he was to point out that someone's shoes needed mending. John couldn't help but notice that several of the inn's other patrons were also shooting suspicious looks in the direction of Wright and his friends.

"Never mind, they won't hear us all the way over here," John told Duncan and George.

He took a sip of his drink, averting his gaze from the Loyalist party. It was hard to know what to think of Duncan's insult. Loyalist or not, Wright had always seemed a decent enough fellow—it was odd to think of him now as some sort of enemy.

Putting such thoughts aside, John lowered his mug and reached for the cartoon, lifting it near the candle for a better look. "Now, what do you think this could mean?" he asked. "I've been puzzling over it night and day but still can't make head nor tails of it."

George chuckled. "Perhaps you should show it to your father. It seems much like one of his treasure maps, does it not?"

John knew George meant no ill by his lighthearted comment, but nonetheless, he felt a flash of annoyance. This note was a very different matter from his father's imaginary treasure clues. Wasn't it?

"Perhaps you're right," he muttered, reminded of the extra work he'd found waiting for him this week due to his father's distraction. "For all I know, this piece of paper could mean as little as that infernal medallion Father has been chasing about all his life, and our ancestors before him. If I haven't figured this one out by now, I'm unlikely to do so after wasting even more time and energy on it."

Feeling frustrated by the entire matter, he impulsively

tossed the paper aside. "Look out!" Duncan exclaimed, grabbing for it as it fluttered dangerously close to the candle's flame. "You nearly set it afire!"

He quickly tamped out the tiny fingers of flame already eating away at the fiber. Only the edges had been affected, causing little harm to the letter. But Duncan's eyes widened as he glanced at it.

"Look!" Duncan exclaimed. "More writing!"

"What are you talking about?" John grabbed the paper from him. Then he gasped. "You're right! There's a bit of writing along this side that wasn't there before!"

George looked confused. "What do you mean? Writing cannot just appear on paper like that."

"Yes, it can." John pulled the candle toward him. "My father has taught me of such things—a few years ago he even showed me how it is done. If one writes a message using certain substances, such as milk or the juice of an onion, the words will dry invisibly, but if you later expose them to heat they will appear again. Don't you see? That is what Alden was trying to tell me as he died! He said I should put the heat on the—" Suddenly realizing that his voice had grown louder with excitement, John glanced over at Wright and his friends and lowered it. "That I should 'put the heat on the Loyalists,'" he finished. "Now, let us see if this works. . . ."

He carefully held the sheet of paper as close to the flame as he could without setting it afire again. Moments later, more words appeared on the back of the cartoon. The faintly visible lines read:

Poor Richard wrought the governor's shame
when one man's "true sentiments" did inflame;
Spy ye one 'tis not the same
whence to all Patriots such news came.

"Incredible!" Duncan whispered, leaning farther over the table for a better look. "Now *that* sounds more like a clue!"

"Indeed. But what does it mean?" John stared at the lines thoughtfully. "Poor Richard surely indicates the great Patriot Mr. Franklin, the author of this very cartoon."

"It does?" George wrinkled his brow.

Duncan nodded. "Franklin published *Poor Richard's*

Almanack," he explained. "And the bit about 'the governor's shame' could refer to the Hutchinson Letters affair of this past year."

"What?" Now both John and George stared at him in confusion.

Duncan sighed impatiently. "For a pair of so-called Patriots, you two pay no attention whatsoever to current affairs!" he complained. "Do you not recall when Governor Hutchinson's private letters were printed in the *Boston Gazette*?"

"I suppose," John said, vaguely recollecting the scandal, though George continued to look perplexed. "What of it?"

"The letters were addressed to the government back in England, asking them to send more soldiers to Boston to keep us in line," Duncan explained. "It is said that an anonymous Patriot sent the letters to Mr. Franklin, who has lived in England these past ten years or so but remains a great champion of the colonies. After reading their contents, Mr. Franklin thought his friends over here should know about the governor's intentions. He sent the letters to them on condition they not be made public. However, they ended up printed for all to see in the *Gazette*, causing outrage among

Bostonians—and all Patriots." He glared at his friends. "All Patriots who were paying attention, that is. In any case, Hutchinson was forced back to England, and when the British accused several innocent men of the leak, Franklin owned up to it himself."

"All right, then," John said. "But what does that have to do with . . . Oh!" He jumped, startled, and quickly covered the clue with his arm as a shadow fell across the table. Looking up, he was relieved to see that it was only his sister Alice. "Oh, it's you."

"What are you boys doing?" Alice smiled and sat down beside John.

"Just this—look what we found!" John had showed her the letter earlier, but now he explained about the invisible ink. "We've deduced so far that it has something to do with Mr. Franklin, and the governor's letters . . ."

As John spoke, Alice scanned the lines. She had learned to read at dame school, but unlike many girls—including her older sisters—she still read often for pleasure.

"Oh, I know what the second line is about!" she exclaimed. "See? One man's 'true sentiments'—that must refer to the book called *The True Sentiments of America*. It contains writings by different people, among them Mr. Samuel Adams." She pointed to the original note. "Perhaps that's the meaning of the initials S. A. here."

"Alice, you are brilliant!" Duncan cried admiringly. "That makes perfect sense, as Mr. Adams is rumored to be the one who caused the letters to be published in the *Gazette*."

John's mind jumped back to the imposing figure he'd seen stand up before the crowd in the Old South Meeting House so many months earlier. Could the message in front of them have really originated with the great Samuel Adams himself?

George was shaking his head. "All right, but what does any of this *mean*?"

John stared down at the lines. And suddenly, there it was—the answer, as clear as if it, too, had been written in invisible ink and just appeared before him. He felt a thrill of excitement rush through his body—the same type of thrill as he got from galloping a fine horse at top speed.

"I've got it!" he said. "'*Whence to all Patriots such news came*'—news! Do you see? It must refer to the *Boston Gazette* itself! The message is sending us to an answer hidden in the *Gazette*!"

Four

During the first flush of excitement in the tavern that evening, the puzzle had seemed all but solved. But a day or two later John found himself still trying to work out what to do next. He felt certain he was right about the clue pointing them toward the *Gazette*. Beyond that, he still felt lost. Were they supposed to look for something that had been printed in the newspaper on a certain date? Was it to have been written by Samuel Adams himself, or were the initials simply a note to the identity of the individual clue's creator?

He was still thinking about it as he mucked out Liberty's stall one evening before bringing her in for the night. By now he knew the lines of the clue by heart, and he recited them to himself under his breath as he worked.

"Whence to all Patriots such news came," he muttered. "Whence. Whence . . ."

Suddenly he let out a shout and straightened up so

quickly that he nearly dropped his fork. A cat that had been sniffing for mice in the next stall bolted for the door, but John paid it no mind.

"That's it!" he cried. He had the answer!

Early the next morning John and his two friends prepared to set off for Boston. Liberty snorted and tossed her head as John led her out of the stable and brought her to a stop in the courtyard.

"Almost ready to go," John said. "Doing all right, George?"

"Aye." George had just led his horse out as well. He was riding John's father's gelding, the heavy-shouldered liver chestnut usually referred to as Big Red.

"Are you certain of this?" Duncan asked, gazing down at the others from the saddle, his cane already tied behind him. Due to his handicap, Duncan was not as strong a rider as the other two. But he could ride well enough, and to be on the safe side John had put him on the horse he called Salem after the town where he had been foaled. Salem was a fat, roan gelding with a kind temperament and a very smooth gait, and John was confident that he would give Duncan no trouble.

"I am as certain as I can be," John replied, checking his

mare's girth. "What other explanation is there? The clue has to be pointing us not toward the paper specifically, but toward the *offices* of the *Gazette*. That must be where this treasure is hidden! We will find it and give it to the Patriot cause as Alden instructed."

George finished adjusting his tack and swung into the saddle. "I just hope you are right," he said. "It was no easy matter to get away for two days—my father was not happy to see me taking off when the bean harvest is not yet in."

"The bean harvest already?" Duncan shook his head. "It is strange to think that September has arrived so quickly."

"Only barely arrived." George smiled over at him. "It is just September the first, after all."

"Never mind." John tightened Liberty's girth one more notch, causing her to dance in place and snake her head around with ears flat back. Ignoring that, John vaulted into the saddle. "The beans can wait another day or two. Let us be off!"

The rather cool, damp morning soon mellowed into a pleasant day, warm and sunny with a hint of a breeze. The three young men chatted as they rode through the familiar countryside between Concord and Boston. Many people were out harvesting their fields or just enjoying the weather. However, John couldn't help but notice that there seemed to be more than the usual number of British regulars on the roads heading toward Boston.

"What is this?" Duncan wondered aloud after they'd passed yet another group of the red-coated soldiers—commonly referred to by the Patriots as lobsters or lobsterbacks—marching along the road. "I've never seen so many lobsterbacks about in a single morning."

John shrugged and checked the sun's position trying to estimate how soon they would reach Boston. "Who knows?" he said. "Perhaps they're expecting trouble due to all the grumbling over the harsh way Governor Gage has been enforcing the Port Act."

George nodded soberly. "Perhaps. My father is worried that if things go on as they've been lately, it could mean all-out war before long."

"War with England?" John didn't like to think of the possibility. Uncovering Patriot codes and arguing politics was one matter; true war was quite another. "I'm sure things won't go that far. Now take the left fork up ahead—I know a shortcut."

✵ ✵ ✵

Once the three friends had arrived in Boston, it didn't take long to locate the offices of the *Boston Gazette and Country Journal*, located on Queen Street.

"Now what?" George asked, squinting up at the tall, narrow frame building with weatherboard siding.

"We could just go inside and ask." Duncan suggested uncertainly. "It is common knowledge that Edes and Gill are promoters of the Patriot cause. Perhaps they will know what we seek."

John hesitated. Normally he valued Duncan's suggestions greatly. Somehow, though, it didn't seem right simply to march into the offices of the popular weekly and start questioning the publishers about a treasure he didn't even know for sure existed. Besides that, there seemed to be a lot of activity going on at the offices at the moment. Men rushed in and out, most of them looking rather wild-eyed and frenzied. John wondered if this was merely the normal hustle and bustle of a busy press, or if perhaps some great piece of news was just being reported.

"Let's just take a look around first," he decided. "Come, we can tie the horses out of the way and then return."

"What *exactly* are we looking for?" George asked as he dismounted.

John bit his lip. He'd been pondering the same question off and on all through the ride. "Something that is 'not the same' I suppose," he said, referring to the third line in the clue. "'. . . spy ye one 'tis not the same.' A different type of press, perhaps, or something about one of the rooms or doors."

But that seemed easier said than done. After tying their horses down the block, the boys returned to find the newspaper offices in even more of an uproar than a few minutes earlier. In fact, the activity seemed to be increasing so rapidly that it soon became obvious to John that there would be no sneaking in unnoticed that day.

"We could wait until everyone leaves for the evening," George proposed. "Surely we can find a way in then." He cracked his knuckles, shooting an appraising glance at the nearest window.

"It's getting later all the time, with no sign of anyone going home," John pointed out. "For all we know, this commotion could go on all night." He took a few steps to one side as a gaunt, older man rushed past, barely seeming to notice John and the others standing there as he headed for the front door shouting something about the Sons of Liberty.

Duncan stared after the old man curiously. "What was he saying?" he asked. "It sounds as if—"

"I've got it!" John cried, interrupting him. Stepping out of the old man's way had brought him within sight of a section of the building's facade previously hidden from view, and something had just caught his eye. He pointed to the weatherboard. "Look there," he said, excitement building within him. "See that board about eight feet up? It looks as if it has recently been replaced—it is a slightly different color than the rest. Could that possibly be what we are seeking?"

Duncan's face lit up. "'Spy ye one 'tis not the same,'" he quoted. "It does make sense!"

George shook his head, looking confused. "A bit of weatherboard?" he said. "How could there be a treasure hiding there?"

"It might not be a treasure." John squinted up at that board, more certain than ever that they'd solved the puzzle. "It could be another clue. My father says that the greatest treasures are often hidden at the end of a trail of several clues, so as to make them more difficult for just anyone to find."

He felt a twinge at the mention of his father. What would Thomas say if he knew of his son's current quest? Would he feel proud—or left out?

He put such thoughts out of his mind as he and his friends discussed how to go about reaching the odd board. None of them wanted to be noticed. But they soon deduced that not one of the dozens of men rushing in and out of the building was paying them any mind at all.

"Why not make a try?" George grinned. "If anyone scolds us, we shall simply have to return later after all. No harm done. Now come—John, if you and I can hoist Duncan upon our shoulders, he should be able to reach that board with those nimble fingers of his. . . ."

Moments later, Duncan was balanced precariously upon the shoulders of his two larger, stronger friends. "Argh," John grumbled, shifting his weight. "For such a skinny fellow, Duncan, you are awfully heavy!"

Duncan paid him no attention. "It's on quite tightly," he said, scrabbling at the siding boards. "But there is a bit of a bump. If I can only wriggle it a bit, like this—a-ha! Got it!"

The other two, with some relief, carefully lowered him to the ground. Rubbing his shoulder, John leaned closer and saw that Duncan was holding what appeared to be a small, plainly styled snuffbox. He handed it to John with a pleased smile.

"That's it?" George looked dubious, but then he shrugged. "All right, then. Let's have it open and see what we've—"

"Listen, men!" a loud shout interrupted him. "The story has just been confirmed by post rider. We cannot let those regulars get away with this! Who is ready to march with me?"

A hearty collection of "ayes" rang out. Glancing over, John saw that a small crowd had gathered near the front door of the newspaper offices while he and his friends had been busy with their task. The fervent-looking young man who had spoken was standing before them clenching both fists above his head.

"What's all this then?" John muttered, tucking the snuffbox away in his clothes for safe-keeping as he moved a bit closer to the crowd.

George was a few steps ahead of his friends. "What is happening?" he called out to the gathered men. "What story was confirmed?"

"Haven't ye heard, boy?" a wild-eyed man near the back of the crowd cried out. "It's the infernal regulars—they're after our gunpowder!"

"That's right," the man at the front called. "General Gage and his men have seized the stores at Winter Hill in Charlestown. It happened just this morning."

"I heard they're headed to Cambridge next!" someone yelled from within the crowd. "And irregulars are marching from all over Massachusetts to stop them!"

"Well, I heard the British Army is massing troops outside of Boston and plans to open fire on any Patriot it can find!" someone else shouted.

"It'll be the Boston Massacre all over again," the man at the front cried, pumping his fist. "Let's be certain to fight back harder this time, boys!"

"Right! If the Loyalists want war, let us give it to them!" another man bellowed.

As further cries rang out and men started hurrying off down the street, John felt his heart beating faster. Was this another step closer to war with England? Despite all the talk and speculation of the past months, such a thing had always seemed impossible. But the tide appeared to be changing.

John knew only one thing for certain—if it came to war, he was ready to fight for the colonies.

Five

A few days later, John looked up from polishing the buckle on a bridle to see George and Duncan entering the harness shop. "Is there any more news of Thursday's raid and march?" he asked them eagerly. John was anxious for any detail about what they had witnessed in Boston, and news was often slow to reach Concord.

George shook his head. "Nothing of importance," he replied. "It seems the rumors of war were greatly exaggerated. General Gage has backed off with his tail tucked between his legs." He chuckled and rubbed his hands together. "I am sure he wasn't expecting the response he got!"

"Indeed," Duncan agreed. "I have heard there were groups of irregulars marching from towns outside Massachusetts as well!" As he spoke, he moved over to the pile of harness on the table and sorted through it. "Have you need of help today?" he asked.

"Yes, thanks. Father is off somewhere again and several

customers wish to pick up their goods on Monday," John said. "But first—are you not forgetting something?" With a grin, he pulled out the snuffbox they'd found at the *Gazette* offices.

"Oh, I *had* forgotten! Lucky you didn't lose it in all the excitement," Duncan said.

"Lucky for all of us." John said with a laugh. "Now let's just see if it was worth the trouble." With his friends watching, he pried open the lid, which had been bent and twisted securely shut. Within, he saw a small silver key and a slip of paper.

"What does it say?" George asked eagerly. "Is that a key to a treasure chest?"

John unfolded the paper, which held two lines of script. "'Mr. Livingston, Roxbury,'" he read aloud. "'*Vox Clamantis in Deserto.*'"

"Is that Latin?" George wrinkled his nose. John knew that his friend had not been fond of the little bit of Latin they'd all had to learn in school.

"May I?" Duncan reached for the paper. When John handed it over, he quickly scanned it. "It *is* Latin," he said. "I think it means, er . . ." He paused, reading over the line once more. "Something very like, 'One voice crying in the wilderness.' At least I believe that to be correct, more or less."

John glanced at Duncan, impressed. His friend might be weak of limb, but he was forever proving himself powerful of intellect. More than once he'd caught his friend at the tavern poring over some book or other, sometimes in the company of John's sister Alice. In fact, John had often thought that Duncan and Alice were like peas in a pod in that way—neither could get enough of books or learning. John himself much preferred educating himself through action and activity, but he could appreciate their patient study. And he was now very glad of it, as it saved them tracking down some Latin schoolmaster to translate the clue for them.

"*'One voice crying in the wilderness,'*" John repeated, feeling a twinge of familiarity somewhere in the recesses of his mind. "I know I have heard that phrase before."

"But what does it mean? It does not sound like much of a clue." George grabbed the paper from Duncan and turned it over. "Do you suppose there could be another invisible message written on here?"

"Perhaps." John reached for the oil lamp sitting on a shelf nearby. "Let us find out."

Some ten minutes and a singed corner later, all three friends were satisfied that there was no invisible writing on the paper. "That is that, I suppose," Duncan said with a sigh. "The clue must lie in the visible words."

"And in this." John picked up the key, which still lay in the snuffbox. He examined it closely, but there were no words or marks on it that might indicate its purpose.

George was looking over John's shoulder at the key. "Perhaps all we need is to find the door or container that this key might open. So let us ride for Roxbury and see what we might find!" He sounded ready to leave at that very moment.

John was tempted to go along with this plan. A treasure for the Patriot cause could be so close! But he forced himself to shake his head. "There is no point in that," he said. "Not until we figure out more of what this means."

Duncan nodded. "Let us all continue to think on it," he said. "We puzzled out the other riddle—I am confident we can solve this one as well."

George looked disappointed. But he shrugged agreeably.

"All right, then," he said. "But if you should change your minds on that, you need only say the word!"

"And I also saw Mrs. Smith at the inn, and she was telling me that the new Continental Congress shall meet in Philadelphia within the week," Alice said.

Several days had passed since John and his friends had found the message in the snuffbox. It was suppertime, and the Gates family was gathered around the table near the fire.

"Oh, dear." Elizabeth shook her head, looking vaguely concerned. "I do hope that will not start more trouble with England."

John looked up from his food with a frown. "It was *England* that started the trouble," he pointed out. "None of this would be happening if not for the Intolerable Acts and the other injustices before them."

Alice nodded and looked over at Elizabeth. "You are sounding suspiciously like a Loyalist, sister. Do you believe we in the colonies should exist only at the pleasure of the king? Do you think the king's governor should be allowed to appoint all other government positions or that the regulars should be housed in our barns and outsheds at will?"

"Oh, I do not think of such matters at all." Elizabeth laughed and waved one hand as if shooing away a fly. "Now, would you like some more meat, Father?"

"No, thank you," Thomas growled, glancing up from his meal with a frown. "What I would *like* is to hear no more of politics while I am eating. It is most tiresome and certainly bad for the digestion." His gruff words caused even the twins, who had been involved in their own little conversation at the far end of the table, to fall silent.

John met Alice's eye and shrugged. Looking frustrated, she turned away to stoke the fire, and John returned his eyes to his meal and his thoughts to the clue from the snuffbox. What could it possibly mean?

Since their meeting in the harness shop, he and his friends had come no closer to finding the answer, but in the meantime much else had happened. After the incident in Charlestown, which some were now calling the Powder Alarm, the Massachusetts militia had started asking for volunteers to join the Minutemen, a group of soldiers who could be ready at a moment's notice to respond to any threat. George had been one of the first in Concord to sign up, to John's initial surprise; he'd always thought his friend a casual Patriot at best, disinterested in much having to do with the conflict with England.

"Perhaps that was true before," George had said when questioned. "But the king has been overstepping his bounds a bit too much for my taste lately. I am a Patriot in mind and heart, and I intend to prove that with my life if needed."

John and Duncan were in agreement with that. Both wished they could follow their friend's lead and join the Minutemen themselves. John had gone so far as to speak with one of the local militia officers. But upon hearing of his duties as a post rider, the officer had assured him that such a job was equally important.

Duncan hadn't even bothered to try to volunteer. Not only did his physical limitations stand in his way, but his family as well. His father, a hardworking wheelwright, seemed convinced that the current mood of rebellion would blow over, just as it had at the time of the Stamp Act, the Sugar Act, and various other outrages in the past. Therefore, he was determined to remain neutral in the conflict and wished his entire family to do the same, much to Duncan's frustration.

"My father can try to tell me what to do," he told John and George with great passion after one particularly heated exchange with his father. "But he cannot force me to feel the same way he does!"

John thought of that as he gazed at his father now. Was Thomas, too, a neutral? John had never asked him. As exasperated as John grew sometimes with Thomas's dreamy and unreliable nature, he had always respected his father's intelligence and therefore assumed him to be sympathetic to the Patriot cause. Was that assumption misplaced? Could this be yet one more thing standing between father and son?

To distract himself from such unsettling thoughts, he quickly returned his mind to the latest clue. The words of the second line kept running through his head, infuriating in its vague familiarity. *Vox Clamantis in Deserto.* What was the clue trying to tell him?

John spent several more days puzzling over the clue with no success. Then one day he accompanied his father to the center of the village to deliver some heavy pieces of harness. The two of them had just dropped off their loads and were heading toward the inn to visit Mary when they noticed a great commotion on the green in front of the church.

"What is going on there?" John wondered aloud, noting that there had to be at least two dozen men gathered. There were occasional bursts of cheers, a dog was barking with excitement, and several small boys were hopping up and down at the back of the crowd trying to get a view of whatever was happening.

Thomas frowned. "I think we'd best find out. Come along, son."

Hurrying over, they pushed their way to the front of the group of spectators. Only then could they see the pathetic figure of a man covered from head to foot in sticky pine tar. The tarred man was crying out in pain and struggling to escape from several laughing captors.

"Hold him still, boys!" someone cried out with a wild cackle.

"Sims," Thomas muttered, recognizing his voice.

Sure enough, it was Mr. Sims who was moving forward with a large basket brimming with poultry feathers. Two of his sons were in the crowd as well, including the one who'd fancied Mary.

The tarred figure twisted and cried out again, trying to

get away as Sims gleefully upended the basket over him. Feathers poured down upon him, most sticking to the hot tar all over his body and the rest drifting away in the early autumn breeze.

"That'll teach 'im!" one of the Sims boys cried out. "He'll not soon mess with the Patriots again!"

"What is going on here?" Thomas yelled, sounding angry. "Is that not our own neighbor, Henry Norris? What has he done to deserve this treatment?"

John was doubly surprised by his father's outburst. First of all, he never would have expected such a reaction from him. Tarring and feathering might not be an official punishment, but it was not uncommon. If anything, he might have expected Thomas simply to move on and mind his own business.

Secondly, he was startled to realize that his father was correct in the identification of the victim. The young man's facial features were so obscured by the materials of his humiliation, as well as his own tears, that John had not recognized him. But he had been in school with Henry's younger brother and knew Henry himself as a studious boy with a quick laugh who had left town to attend the local university down in Boston about a year earlier.

Sims scowled at Thomas. "What business is it of yours, Gates?" he spat out. "We are dealing with a treasonous Loyalist, that's all."

"But I'm not!" Henry cried out, the words choked off with a sob. "I'm not! I'm only here visiting my family, that's all. I didn't do any of the terrible things you're saying!"

"Indeed!" the younger Sims son said sarcastically. "Well, my brother has it on good authority that you aided the lobsterbacks in the Powder Alarm. And I will certainly trust the word of my brother over that of some treasonous Loyalist spy!"

Thomas was shaking his head, his expression grim. "What has this town come to?" he said loudly. "I never would have expected to see my own neighbors accuse and humiliate one of our own like this, with no apparent proof. And a mere boy, no less!"

"Think as you like, Gates," someone John couldn't see shouted from the crowd. "This 'boy' is more than old enough to commit treason!"

Most of the others gathered shouted out their agreement. As John and his father watched, they dragged Henry off and forced him to straddle a rail which the elder Sims son and a few other men then lifted on their shoulders.

"Let the parade begin!" Mr. Sims cried to the cheering crowd.

Thomas turned away, shaking his head. "Let us go home, son," he said to John. "I do not wish to witness this. Poor Henry must be wishing he'd stayed down there at Harvard and never thought to return home. *Veritas*, indeed."

John followed his father toward their house. Part of him was still disturbed by what he'd just witnessed. Loyalist or not, it was hard to observe such treatment.

But another part of him was filled with excitement. His father's words had stirred something in his brain. He was almost certain he'd just figured out the newest clue!

Six

"What is it?" George sounded distracted as he sighted down his caliver. "I am due at shooting practice with the Minutemen in a few minutes."

"Let us walk you there," John said. "I have important news."

"Yes," Duncan put in, leaning upon his cane. "And he refused to tell me what it is until we were all together."

John chuckled at Duncan's disgruntled look. "All right, I can tell you now," he said. George shouldered his musket, and the three of them began walking in the direction of the village green. "I have finally remembered why that Latin phrase sounded familiar. It is the motto of Dartmouth College, that new Indian school up in New Hampshire! I remember Alice mentioning it; as you know, she is always filling her mind with thoughts of higher education." He was rather proud of himself for remembering that at last. It had been his father's mention of Harvard and its own Latin motto that had nudged the memory out of the recesses of his mind.

"Very interesting!" Duncan looked thoughtful. "But does that mean the next clue is in New Hampshire colony?"

George frowned and shook his head. "That seems a long way to travel on this sort of quest, especially in such dangerous times. Besides, what of the reference to Roxbury? Most likely, it refers to the town of Roxbury here in Massachusetts."

John had to admit that he knew no more about that than they did. "Still, at least it is progress," he said aloud. "If we talk it through with this new knowledge, perhaps we can figure it out."

"You shall have to start without me." George's gaze was fixed on the village green just ahead. Some two dozen of his fellow Concord Minutemen were already gathered there. "See you later."

As he hurried off to join his regiment, John and Duncan hung back and watched from a distance. Taking a seat on a stone wall outside the blacksmith's shop, they continued their discussion to the sounds of marching orders.

"Perhaps this Mr. Livingston, whoever he may be, lives

in Roxbury and holds the treasure? Maybe he's associated with the college."

"Perhaps," John said.

He glanced toward the practicing militiamen. George and the others were standing in formation, going through the process of preparing their weapons to fire.

As John watched, the commanding officer raised his hand. "Ram down the cartridge and present, men!" the man called out. "Ready, and fire! Fire until British tea pours out of their sorry hides!"

"Tea!" John exclaimed, the word nearly lost amidst the blast of gunfire.

Duncan blinked at him. "Has a sudden thirst come upon you?" he joked.

John shook his head impatiently. "I've just figured it out," he said. "The *Dartmouth*—that was the name of one of the tea ships involved in the incident last December. That must be where the clue is pointing us! Not to the college, but to the *ship!*"

"Interesting." Duncan sounded slightly dubious. "But what help is that in knowing what to do next? The ship *Dartmouth* is no more located in Roxbury than is the college."

"True enough." John shrugged. "But it seems more than coincidence, does it not?"

"I suppose so." Duncan paused to think. "Could some portion of the tea brought over on the *Dartmouth* itself be the treasure?" he suggested after a moment. "And the rest of the clue a way to indicate that it is now hidden with this Mr. Livingston? It would make some sort of sense, given the value of tea. . . ."

John shook his head. "Not possible. I was there that night, remember?" He smiled at the memory. "There was not a leaf of tea remaining on the *Dartmouth* when we were through. Unless someone dragged it from the bottom of the harbor, it cannot be the treasure." He shrugged. "But I am beginning to think that both you and George are partly right. It may be time to make a trip to Roxbury and see about finding this Mr. Livingston."

Unfortunately, neither Duncan nor George was able to make the journey to Roxbury. George was needed for more maneuvers with the militia, and Duncan's father was growing more and more officious over his son's free time, insisting with great mistrust that he not spend so much of it with "admitted radicals" such as George and John.

For his part, John wasn't entirely certain what his father would think of his quest. Since the tarring-and-feathering incident, the two of them had not mentioned politics in each others' presence again, and John found himself glad he'd not mentioned this odd quest he had stumbled upon to him.

Despite these worries, John had no trouble inventing a post delivery as an excuse to ride for Roxbury within a few days. Liberty was in fine form, surging forward at a trot as soon as John had mounted and taking every opportunity after that to break into a brisk canter. By late afternoon, John was riding into the hilly village of Roxbury.

Spying a livery stable at the edge of town, he stopped there and left Liberty to eat, drink, and rest. "Shall you be needing a fresh horse for your return journey, sir?" inquired the fresh-faced stableboy, who couldn't have been much older than John's younger sisters.

Smiling a bit at being called "sir," John shook his head. "My mare will be fine after a rest," he said, patting Liberty on her sweaty neck. "I shall return for her shortly. In the meantime, do you know of a man called Livingston in these parts?"

"Oh, yes, sir," the stableboy replied over his shoulder as he led Liberty off toward a water trough. "Mr. Livingston runs the shop on Centre Street. Is that who you want, sir?"

"Yes, I think so. Thank you." Tossing the boy a coin in thanks, John turned and headed out.

By asking a few passersby, he soon found the shop in question. The name displayed over the door indicated that the proprietor's name was indeed Livingston.

Taking a deep breath, John pushed open the shop door and entered. The musty scents of tea, spices, and mildew assaulted his nose. Once his eyes had adjusted to the dim light within, he saw that the shop consisted of a small room lined with shelves containing imported goods of every conceivable type, from molasses to carrots. The place was deserted apart from a short, stocky man standing behind the counter writing busily in a ledger.

"Good afternoon, young man," the shopkeeper said, looking up briefly at John before returning his attention to his book. "Let me know if I can be of service."

John cleared his throat and glanced around. Now that he

was here, he still had no idea what to do. Somehow, he'd hoped that just finding Mr. Livingston would provide some further clue—a portrait of the ship *Dartmouth* hanging on the wall of the shop, perhaps. But no such clue made itself evident.

"Er, excuse me, sir," he said. "Uh, *Vox Clamantis in Deserto.*"

Mr. Livingston looked up again, squinting at John. "I beg your pardon?"

Feeling rather foolish, John took a step backward. For a moment the man's dubious expression made him consider turning and leaving the shop immediately. Still, perhaps it was only that the man hadn't heard him properly . . .

"*Vox Clamantis in Deserto?*" he repeated.

He held his breath as the shopkeeper's expression did not waver. For another long moment John was certain he'd made a mistake. It seemed very unlikely that either treasure or clue was to be found there, in a shop full of goods from England.

Then Livingston nodded. "Come along then, young man," he said. "I believe you'll find the merchandise you're seeking is this way."

John followed the man through a door in the back. He

found himself in a tiny room stacked high with old boxes and trunks, many of them padlocked. Livingston lit a single lamp sitting on a shelf by the door and then disappeared back out into the main shop, pulling the door shut behind him.

Staring around in confusion, John wondered what to do now. He pulled out the tiny key that had been hidden with the clue. Was it meant to open one of the boxes or trunks in this room? Which one? There had to be at least four or five dozen altogether!

"Ah, well," he murmured to himself with a shrug. "As George might say, the task won't get started until I start it."

He stepped toward the nearest pile of boxes, ready to begin testing the key in whatever locks he could find. But as he was reaching for the first trunk, a wooden box a little higher up caught his eye. The company name *Davison, Newman, and Co.* stamped on its side was one that had been burned into his mind's eye the previous December, when he had hoisted countless identical boxes. . . .

"That's it!" he blurted out, nearly knocking over the lamp as he leaped toward the box. His heart was thumping wildly in his chest as he looked around the storage room, trying to spot any other boxes bearing the same logo. But there was no other. Only this one tea chest, stamped with the name of the company whose tea John had helped toss over the side of the ship *Dartmouth*!

Pulling the crate from its stack, John set it on the floor and then carefully fitted the key into the lock. It turned easily, and he let out the breath he hadn't even realized he was holding.

The box was empty aside from a musty odor, a few stray tea leaves, and a slip of paper. John picked up the paper, closed and locked the box and returned it to its spot before carrying the paper over to the lamp. By the flickering light, he read what was written.

Those Initial Massacred Five
Shall help we Patriots shift and thrive

Aoccer srcgmhoccer meeg
Ccne in ecgborn brecme

John blinked, shook his head, and then leaned closer to the lamp. But it was not a trick of light. The last two lines remained as indecipherable as when he'd first seen them.

What in the world could it all mean?

Seven

"It's clearly some type of code or cipher," Duncan said the next day.

George let out a snort. "I would not use the word 'clearly' to describe anything about this." He waved his hand at the latest clue, which lay on a large, flat rock between them. The three friends were poring over it in one of the harvested fields on George's family's property. "It makes no sense whatsoever to me!"

John knew how he felt. He was no closer to understanding the note than when he had first seen it. Like Duncan, he had concluded that the second pair of lines had to be written in code. His father had taught him all about such things as a boy, from the Vigenère cipher to the classic Caesar cipher.

"I was thinking that the first two lines might hold some sort of hint as to where to find the key to the code," he told his friends. "The 'massacred five' surely refers to the Boston Massacre a few years back."

George wrinkled his brow. "Do you think the treasure is hidden somewhere in the Old State House in Boston?" he asked. "That's where the Massacre took place, is it not?"

"It seems a logical assumption," John said. "Maybe the coded lines tell us where in the State House to search?" He sighed and rubbed his forehead. "But without a key to the code, we have little chance of ever deciphering it."

Over the course of the next few days, the three friends continued to puzzle over the latest clue whenever they could, John most of all. He stared at the clue so frequently, in fact, that he soon found himself making out its letters in the shapes of the spiky tree braches that were rapidly losing the last of their leaves for the season, hearing the words in the songs that Elizabeth and the twins sang as they worked around the house, and seeing them appear behind his lids whenever he closed his eyes. It was maddening.

"I'm thinking it might be time to accept defeat and ride down to New London again to give this task back to Nathan Hale," he told Duncan one day when the two of them met outside the village barber's, from which Duncan had just emerged. "Surely he will know how to proceed." John hated to admit defeat, but he might be doing the

Patriots a disservice by keeping the clues to himself.

Duncan, however, did not agree. "Will he?" Duncan asked, brushing absently at the wisps of hair on his shoulders. "Are you certain that he is the one who concocted these clues?"

"Not certain at all, no. But if he did not lay the trail himself, it seems at least likely that he has knowledge of who did so." John bit his lip. "The trouble is, I shall have to figure out what to tell Father if I am to leave for so long again. . . ."

As the pair began to walk, Duncan flicked a stone out of their path with his cane. "It may be too soon for that in any case," he said. "Have you showed this clue to your sister Alice?"

"I mentioned it to her once, but she has not yet seen the clue itself," John replied. "I was about to show it to her yesterday, but Mercy came running in, and I had to hide it away again before she could see and start wagging her tongue to Father."

"Well, perhaps you might try again. If nothing else, Alice can help you concoct a reason for needing to ride to Connecticut."

As usual, Duncan was right. Later that day John found Alice working alone over the baking and took the opportunity to show her the clue.

Her face lit up with interest as she scanned the lines. "Oh, a code!" she said, wiping flour from her hands on her apron. "I remember that Father used to talk of such things over the supper table. But where is the key?"

"That's what I'd like to know," John said, glancing over his shoulder to be certain that nobody else was near. He leaned against the edge of the wooden table. "I wonder if the first two lines point to where we might find it. Or perhaps they contain the key themselves. If only I could figure out what they are supposed to mean . . ."

"Let us approach this with logic, John," Alice said, her forehead creased with thought. "Now, the clues so far have appeared to involve Patriot persons and matters. So we might try thinking in that direction."

John glanced at her, impressed. He hadn't really made that connection, but she was correct. The first clue had involved well-known Patriots Benjamin Franklin and Samuel Adams, along with the Hutchinson letters and the Patriot-sympathizing *Boston Gazette*, and then of course the second had evoked the infamous tea ships in Boston Harbor.

"Indeed, there is a pattern," he murmured. "And true to form, this latest clue points to the Boston Massacre."

"Yes, that much is obvious." Alice nodded and paused just long enough to check on the bread. "However, what is the meaning of the reference? In the previous clues, it was required for you to know something of recent events in order to find the answer."

John nodded slowly. "In the first case, it was necessary to be familiar with the matter of the Hutchinson letters as well as knowing that Samuel Adams was said to be responsible for the whole thing. And in the last clue, one had to know that the *Dartmouth,* bearing the same name as the new college, was one of the ships involved in the Destruction of the Tea."

"So what are we expected to know of the Boston Massacre?" Alice wondered aloud, gazing at the words on the paper. "Perhaps that will provide the key to the coded lines below."

John sighed. It could be anything! A newspaper article about the Massacre, something at the site where it occurred. How can we be expected to know where to look?"

"The layer of this trail surely did not wish it to end here," Alice said calmly. "He has provided enough hints to allow you to solve the other clues. Surely there are hints here, too, that we have so far missed. For instance, I am thinking—"

She cut herself off as a sudden commotion arose just outside the kitchen doorway. A second later, one of the twins bounded in.

"How are you doing with the baking, sister?" Humility asked Alice breathlessly. "Elizabeth just sent word that she was delayed in the village, so she wishes me to help you until she returns."

John swallowed back a frustrated groan. Just when Alice had seemed about to say something useful . . .

But Alice merely smiled sweetly at her younger sister. "Thank you, Humility," she said. "But as you can see, John is already here to assist me."

"John?" Humility shot her brother a skeptical look. "What does *he* know of baking? I do not wish our bread to stink of the stable!"

"Mind your mouth, girl," John growled, irritated. "Remember that the stinking stable you mention pays for this bread along with everything else in our household!"

"Easy, both of you." Alice chuckled soothingly. "Now sister, if you wish to help me, perhaps you could go out and clean and refill the water in the henhouse. I have not had the time to do so yet today."

"Fine." Humility shot John one last smirk, then flounced back out of the kitchen.

"There." Alice winked at John. "That should keep her busy for a good while. Now where were we?"

"You were about to tell me how to solve this blasted code," John said. "Now please—enlighten me before Mercy comes in wanting to scrub the floor!"

Alice laughed. "I was just going to say that perhaps the key has something to do with the names of those killed by the regulars that day. See? The clue clearly refers not so much to the event itself as the victims involved—those 'initial massacred five.'"

John let out a gasp as the truth hit him like a set of shod hooves in the midsection. "No!" he cried gleefully. "Not their *names*—their *initials*! Those *initial* massacred five!" His mind raced as he tried to remember all those lessons on coding that he'd learned at his father's knee. "It makes sense—'shift and thrive,' see?" He stabbed a finger at the words on the paper. "Perhaps if we take the initials of the victims and shift them around somehow, it shall give us the answer. The initials are themselves the key—it has to be so!"

Alice laughed at her brother's excitement. "It does make sense," she agreed. "But how are we to find out the names of the victims? Do you think your friend Duncan would know them? He reads quite a lot, and is rather clever . . ."

"No need to ask Duncan." John grinned triumphantly. He had been fairly young at the time of the Massacre, but had heard those five names often enough. "I believe I know them myself. Duncan is not the only clever one around, you know. Wait here while I fetch a quill . . ." John hurried off and soon returned with a quill and ink, along with a blank sheet of paper from one of the harness shop's accounting books. "Now let me think. There was of course the mulatto Crispus Attucks. Another man was named Gray—Samuel Gray, I believe it was . . ." Before long he had written down all five sets of initials: C.A., S.G., S.M., J.C., and P.C.

With Alice's help, he spent the next few minutes poring over the letters, trying to figure out how they might form a key. Not every letter in the gibberish lines was contained within the five sets of initials, so John kept those letters as they were in the original clue. But wherever a letter from one of the five initials did appear, John would substitute it with its pair from the appropriate set of initials. For instance, in the first coded word AOCCER, he substituted the A with C, thereby replacing one of the initials in the name Crispus Attucks with the other. It took a bit of trial and error, particularly involving the letters that were repeated in more than one set of initials such as C and S. For instance, in the first coded word, he tried making it into COAAER and COJJER before finally hitting on COPPER. Some of the other shifts were equally tricky.

Nonetheless, Humility hadn't yet returned from the henhouse before John finally scribbled a pair of decoded lines on the page and smiled triumphantly.

He held up the paper, which now held the lines:

Copper grasshopper sees
Pane in eastborn brease.

Eight

"So?" George called out a few days later as he entered the harness shop, where John and Duncan were awaiting him. "Did you find the next clue at Faneuil Hall as expected?" Due to his increasing Minuteman duties, George had been unable to accompany his friends on their latest adventure in Boston.

"We did," Duncan said eagerly. "It was not easy, either. There were far too many lobsterbacks about."

John nodded. "I knew our next destination as soon as we deciphered the clue about the copper grasshopper," he said. "I immediately thought of the weathervane of Faneuil Hall." He grimaced. "Unfortunately, it took us several tries to locate the next clue, which was etched on a windowsill on the western wall of the building."

"The western wall?" George perched on a stool. "I thought the clue said something about the east."

"As did we, and that was exactly what led to the delay."

John still couldn't believe that he'd taken so long to figure out the correct answer. He could almost hear his father's voice now: *It's all about the details, my boy.* "An eastborn breeze—a wind out of the east—wouldn't have the grasshopper facing eastward. It would have it pointing to the *west!*"

"Ah!" George chuckled. "Whoever laid these clues was clever indeed. So what did you discover?"

John had copied the newest clue onto a piece of paper. He pulled it out now and showed it to George.

In Dorchester there is Enclosed
A message meant for all of those
Within who the thirst for Liberty grows
Much like the roots of fairest rose!

"Dorchester, eh? That isn't far," George said as he read it over. He leaned back on his stool and rested his boots on the worktable, which as usual was littered with half-mended bits of tack. "Perhaps we should ride over there and take a look around. Who knows how long it will take us to figure out the rest of the clue? The ground will freeze before much longer, and then we won't be able to dig up the treasure until the spring thaw. If there is even a treasure to be dug."

Duncan looked dubious. "What is the point of wandering aimlessly around Dorchester?" he said. "We don't know what we would be looking for. I wish Mr. Revere would have taken even the quickest of looks at it," he added with a glance at John.

John nodded in agreement. On their way out of Boston, they'd stopped at Revere's silvershop to tell him of all that had happened since John had seen him last. The silversmith had shaken his head grimly at the mention of Mr. Alden's demise.

"He was a fine young man, a Patriot, and a Freemason with a bright future," Revere had said. "But I am glad to hear that you and your friends have taken over his quest. I had wondered what had become of Hale's message. He will be pleased as well by this news."

"But sir—what is it we are seeking?" John had asked. "The clues have been most unclear on that point."

Revere had shaken his head again. "I am afraid that I do not know the answer to that, my young friend. All I know is that it is something of value that was hidden by members of the Linonian Society in case tensions between Patriots and Loyalists should ever lead to war."

"Linonian Society?" Duncan had repeated curiously.

"Yes. It is one of the debating societies at Yale College in New Haven," Revere had explained. "Nathan Hale was a member while he was at school. Knowing of his great patriotism, the other members entrusted him with the first clue which he in turn was going to give to Alden. From what I understand, the society asked my friend Samuel Adams to let them know when he thought war with England might be near so that they could let Hale know the hunt should begin."

"So Hale wasn't the one who hid this treasure, whatever it is?" John had asked, glad that he hadn't bothered riding to New London for help, as it seemed that would have done him no good at all.

"Not as I understand it," Revere had replied. "In fact, for the purpose of security, I believe that each clue was planted by a different member of the Society. That way, if war came and an individual member of the group was captured by the enemy, he would not be able to lead them to the treasure even if tortured or tricked."

Duncan's eyes had grown wide. "War with England?" he'd said nervously. "Could that ever actually happen? I know things seem bad right now, but . . ."

John had been so wrapped up in the revelation that he was indeed on a treasure hunt of some sort that he had barely been listening. But Duncan's words had snapped him back to focus.

"No man can know what will happen," Revere had said. "That is why it is best to be prepared for anything."

Now, back in the familiar and safe environs of the harness shop, John shivered anew at the memory of Revere's words, not wanting to think too much about what they might mean. But one thing he knew for certain—the meeting with Revere had imbued their quest with a greater sense of urgency than ever before.

Duncan's plea to hold off on a trip to Dorchester was ignored, and so, within the week the three friends found themselves riding for the town. John had been there once or twice delivering mail, and he found the place just as he remembered it—a sleepy little rural town with a handsome church, a handful of businesses, including a chocolate factory, and a scattering of houses and small farms. However, one thing had changed from his memories. Dorchester seemed virtually overrun with British soldiers.

John watched as yet another group marched past in formation, the third such regiment they'd seen in the past twenty minutes. At the same time they moved out of sight over a hill, John spied a towheaded boy of about twelve years wandering along a little farther up the road. Quickly urging Liberty forward, John rode over to the boy, his friends following.

"Is something going on here today?" he called to the boy. "Why are there so many regulars about?"

The boy regarded the three strangers suspiciously. "Who is asking?" he demanded "Be ye Loyalists or Patriots?"

"Patriots!" George responded with such vehemence that his horse shifted its weight nervously. "And proud of it."

The boy visibly relaxed, though some of the disgust and impatience in his expression remained. "It is the Quartering Act," he said. "These lobsterbacks are taking advantage of the Act to lounge about in people's outbuildings, making a mess and helping themselves to all our food and drink."

"And so you have stinking Tories everywhere," George growled. "How can you stand it?"

"How can we not?" The boy shrugged. "There have been grumblings of rebellion, naturally. But nobody wants to bring the full wrath of the king's men upon them by refusing to allow them on their property."

George clenched his fists. "Well, just let some lobster-back try to lodge on my family's farm," he said. "I would make him regret it, Act or no Act!"

Just then a stout woman appeared in the doorway of the nearest house holding a broom in one hand and a baby in the other arm. "William!" she shouted. "What are you about, boy? Get in here!"

The towheaded boy muttered an oath, then ran toward the house without another word. John turned Liberty back down the main road. He was starting to question the wisdom of rushing off to Dorchester as they had. Not only had they no idea what they were searching for, but seeing so many redcoats had only served to remind him that this was no mere game. Much was at stake.

Still, they were here now, so they might as well make the best of it. "Keep your eyes open for anything that might be of interest," he said as his friends rode up on either side of him.

As the horses crested another small hill, George stared down the far side. "I see something of interest," he spat out. "Lobsterbacks making fools of themselves."

Sure enough, a whole group of rowdy redcoats seemed to be having a party at a small farm located at the base of the hill. They were gathered in a wide, flat area between barn and house, laughing raucously, drinking ale, and trampling through what appeared to be the remains of a sizable kitchen garden, completely heedless of the neat, partially painted fence surrounding it. John scowled as he noticed one of the soldiers tossing stones at a pair of draft horses in a nearby paddock, causing the animals to roll their eyes with fear and gallop in circles.

George spat out with disgust. "Have they no respect for a man's property? Perhaps we ought to go down there and teach them a lesson!"

"Wait!" John said quickly. George sounded angry enough that he feared he might actually ride down and start a fight with the redcoats. "I agree that they could use the lesson. But be sensible. There are at least eight or nine of them, and only three of us."

"I do not care," George insisted. "I would gladly take on the entire British army if I—"

"Look!" Duncan blurted out, pointing toward the scene below. "That fence—do you see how it is painted?"

John glanced quickly at the palings, wondering if Duncan had even noticed that George was about to put all of them in fear for their lives. "What of it?" he asked with a touch of impatience. "Perhaps the owner was in the midst of painting it when he was interrupted by those intruding lobsterbacks."

"No, look!" Duncan insisted, his face breaking into a wide grin. "Exactly nine of the pickets are painted in all— five in red and four in white."

Even George had paused in his outrage to stare at Duncan in confusion. "What are you blathering on about?"

Duncan rolled his eyes. "Do you not see?" he said. "The Sons of Liberty often use a flag with nine vertical red-and-white stripes—just like those palings! This is the 'message' we are seeking here in Dorchester!"

John's eyes widened. "You're right!" he cried. "Good eye, Duncan. Only a true Patriot would notice those palings and see a symbol rather than an unfinished bit of work."

"Indeed!" George's anger finally seemed to have faded, replaced by excitement. "Do you suppose the treasure lies buried beneath that fence?"

"No, not the fence," John exclaimed. "Beneath the rosebush—just there. See?" He pointed to a large shrub rose, still clinging to leaves and a few blossoms despite the rapidly cooling autumn weather. "The verse mentioned roses, remember?"

"How lucky that we happened across this spot so quickly!" Duncan said. "We might have ridden for some time in the other direction without benefit."

"But it seems our luck has now run out," John said, his exultant mood deflating as quickly as it had arrived. "The very spot where we wish to dig is positively crawling with regulars. And they appear settled in for a good long while."

"We cannot let them chase us off," George declared. "We just need a plan. . . ."

They moved off the road and into the shelter of a copse of trees. After a few minutes, they had concocted a plan that they all thought might work, though Duncan tried to argue that it was far too dangerous. Once again, though, he was outvoted.

"All right, then," he finally gave in with a sigh. "Tell me once more how it will go?"

"I shall do my best to lure the regulars away by pretending that General Gage is on his way to check on them," John said. "I will tell them he wishes them to muster immediately on the opposite end of town." It had been decided that he should play this role, being the best rider of the three on the fastest horse. "When I have them out of the way, George will move in and dig for the treasure beneath the rose. Meanwhile . . ."

"I shall keep watch and warn George when the soldiers are returning," Duncan took a deep breath. "I suppose it could work. But you will have to be careful, John! Once the lobsterbacks realize you've tricked them—"

"Never mind that," John said. "I won't return here. I'll circle around and await you two at that bridge by the big rock a mile or two out of town. These lobsterbacks will never lay eyes on my face again."

Not seeing any need to delay, they put their plan into action immediately. While his friends remained hidden in the trees, John remounted and rode down the hill to the farm. One of the soldiers spotted him and strolled out to challenge him.

"What is your business here, boy?" he demanded. "Can you not see that we are busy?"

"I—I bring word from General Gage," John stammered out, more nervous than he'd expected to be. "He is on his way . . ." He managed to blurt out the rest of his message. For a moment the soldier looked annoyed, and John feared the plan was a failure almost before it had begun.

Then the redcoat spun on his heel. "Men!" he shouted. "Listen to me!" He repeated what John had told him, to a great deal of consternation and swearing from his comrades. Minutes later, all the soldiers were back in full uniform and getting into marching formation on the road in front of the farm.

"Now, where are we to meet General Gage?" the original man demanded of John.

"Follow me and I will show you." John nudged Liberty into a brisk trot, causing the redcoats to jog in order to keep him in sight.

His heart was pounding as he rode off, not daring to

glance at the wooded area where he knew his friends were hiding. Would this work? What if he encountered more red-coats who knew that his story was false, perhaps mounted themselves? John truly believed that Liberty might be the fastest horse in Massachusetts. But he had no desire to test it against a mob of angry Tories.

Nine

Luck seemed to be smiling on John that day. His part of the plan proceeded without a hitch. Once he'd led the red-coats some four or five miles away from the farm, he spurred Liberty into a gallop and dodged off into a thick area of forest. Within seconds the angry and confused shouts had faded behind him, though he didn't slow below a brisk trot until he had nearly reached the meeting spot.

Once there, he slid down from the saddle and allowed Liberty to graze by the side of the road while he paced nervously. Had he bought enough time for George to find a digging tool and unearth whatever was buried beneath the rose bush? And what if that turned out to be some vast store of treasure too heavy for George and Duncan to dig up and carry off in such a short amount of time? He belatedly realized that they hadn't allowed for that possibility in their hasty plan.

He'd nearly worked himself into a lather when he

finally heard hoofbeats approaching rapidly on the road. Pulling Liberty with him, John ducked behind a stand of trees. To his relief, though, he soon saw that it was his friends. They looked anxious, and for a moment he feared they'd had no success.

But when he stepped into view, George and Duncan both broke into broad grins. "You made it!" George called. "We spent most of the ride debating what we would do if we arrived and found you absent."

"I have had much the same worry over the two of you," John retorted with a laugh. "I was afraid you would not have enough time before the soldiers returned."

"It really did not take that much time at all," Duncan said, pulling his horse to a halt beside John.

George let out a mock groan and rubbed his shoulder. "It is an easy thing for you to say so, my friend," he told Duncan. "You were not the one digging!"

"But did you find anything?" John asked.

George reached into his saddlebags and pulled out a tin box. "Only this," he said. "We were hoping for gold and jewels inside. But there is only another riddle."

Now it was John's turn to groan. "Another?" he said.

Whoever had laid this trail seemed intent on making it difficult. "Let me see it."

George leaned down from the saddle to hand him the box. Opening it, John found a piece of paper containing the verse:

> We are eight strong
> Our voices blend in song
> If ye wish our secret free
> Our kin's verse holds the key
> Be of Independent mind
> Out from our door direction find.

"As usual, it makes little sense that I can figure," George grumbled.

"We worked out the other clues eventually," John said with a sigh. "I suppose we'll simply have to work this one out as well. Come, let's talk it over as we ride for home."

Tucking box and note away in his own saddlebags, he remounted. Liberty was at first resistant to leaving her patch of tasty grass, but at John's insistence she finally turned toward the bridge, albeit with her tail switching irritably and her ears flattened against her head.

"Come on, you ornery mule," John chided her with a laugh. "You should know by now that you'll not intimidate me with your antics."

As Liberty responded by throwing her head between her knees and letting fly with a buck, which John easily rode out, Duncan leaned forward to pat his own mount on the neck. That day his usual choice, Salem, had been sent off with a passing post rider, and so he was riding an old seal bay mare John usually called Granite after her enormous, blocklike head, and rather stubborn and slow nature.

"I wish to thank you, Granny, for not acting like that," Duncan said, clearly only half joking. "You may not be very fast and your trot may jostle me until I fear my insides will end up on the outside, but at least you do not try to kill me on purpose."

Soon John had Liberty in hand again, and the three friends rode off down the road at a leisurely walk. John had left the clue near the top of his saddlebag so he would be able to refer to it if necessary as he rode. But he was able to remember the first couple of lines without doing so.

"'Eight strong, our voices blend in song,'" he recited.

"Do you suppose that could refer to some sort of choir?"

"I don't know," Duncan put in. "That almost seems too easy. Previous clues all required more—"

"There they are!" a voice rang out from some distance behind them.

John gasped and glanced back. On the road, just coming around the bend by the bridge, were at least half a dozen redcoats—on horseback!

"Run!" George cried.

"Get the rotten rascals!" another soldier howled out as all three boys urged their horses into a gallop.

John's heart pounded in his throat as he felt Liberty dig in and pick up speed. Her hooves flew over the road, barely seeming to touch down at all. John had little doubt she could outrun the soldiers. But what about his friends— especially Duncan?

He glanced back over his shoulder to check. George was mounted that day on a young black gelding and seemed fine so far. But Granite was already dropping behind the other two a bit, her lumbering stride no match for the younger, faster horses. Duncan was clinging to her mane, his face white and frightened.

John had to do something. The soldiers, though at least thirty lengths behind at the moment, were likely to be aboard far fresher mounts; they would no doubt catch up before long. Glancing forward, he tried desperately to remember every detail of the roads just ahead. He couldn't afford a mistake now. . . .

Then he asked Liberty to slow her pace slightly. At first she fought him, flinging her head skyward to escape the bit while surging forward faster than ever. But finally he regained control, holding her back until the other two horses had caught up, then steering her over beside George's gelding.

"I have an idea," he shouted, praying that his friend could hear him over the horses' hooves and the whipping wind about them. "You two gallop on ahead and take the right-hand fork at the old oak tree. I'll drop back and go left."

George glanced over at him, his expression grim. But then he glanced at Duncan, who was still clinging for dear life to his horse's mane, and nodded. "Be careful," George called back to John.

"I will. Wait for me behind the church in Waltham."

John didn't bother waiting for a response. He slowed Liberty even more, bringing her down to an easy canter. Ahead, he saw Duncan glance back in confusion. But George shouted and waved him on, and their two horses soon disappeared around the next turn in the road.

The shouts of the redcoats and the thundering of their horses' hooves were rapidly gaining on John. He glanced back, ignoring the shiver of terror he felt as he got a clear look at the men's furious faces. Would this work?

There wasn't much time to ponder it. Soon the quickest of the redcoats' horses was only a dozen lengths behind, then ten, and then only five. . . . When the lead horse, a lithe chestnut, was barely three lengths behind, John finally urged Liberty on a bit faster. The mare jumped forward as if she'd been waiting for such a signal, extending her stride so rapidly that she soon opened up another three or four lengths on their pursuers.

John looked forward, gauging the distance remaining to the fork in the road. Thanks to the hilly, partially wooded landscape, the road meandered like a cow trail. How far ahead were his friends by now? Would it be enough?

Finally Liberty galloped around the base of a hillock

and reached an open stretch of road. The fork lay at the end of this section, the right-hand track leading off along the bank of a windy creek and the left-hand option rising steeply into an area of cropland and small isolated farms. John let out a small sigh of relief when he saw that his friends were nowhere in sight.

"Let's go, girl!" he shouted as Liberty neared the fork, crouching down and steering her to the left. He peeked back, praying that none of the soldiers would catch on to the trick and go the other way. . . .

They did not. All of them urged their horses on after John and Liberty, sweeping three or four across up the left-hand fork. John faced forward again, smiling grimly. *That's lobsterbacks for you,* he thought. *All that marching in formation makes it impossible for them to think as individuals!*

After that quick thought, all his focus went to riding. When concocting this plan he hadn't thought much further than this point, assuming that he and Liberty would lead the soldiers on a merry chase and lose them when they pleased.

But a three or four miles later, he had come to realize that it might not be that easy. Liberty was indeed faster than any of the horses chasing her, but she'd made a long trip already earlier that day. Though her stride never faltered, John could sense her beginning to tire. Her breathing was becoming labored, and she was coated in a sheen of sweat despite the cool temperature. Even she wouldn't be able to go on much longer.

John glanced back, the panicky fingers of desperation clutching at his heart and making his breath catch in his throat. What was he going to do now? If those soldiers caught him . . . But, no. He couldn't think about that. He had to figure out a new plan.

By now they were galloping along a broad, straight stretch of dirt track. On one side lay a field of recently harvested corn, and on the other an uncultivated meadow separated from the road by a high fieldstone wall.

Glancing in one direction and then the other, John knew what he had to do. The wall to the right went on ahead as far as one could see; there would be no getting around it quickly. It had to be at least four feet high—much higher than most riders would dare to jump.

But we have jumped that height and more, you and I, haven't we girl? he thought, glancing down at Liberty's sweat-soaked withers and neck. An image flashed through his head—himself and Liberty galloping about in the fields outside of town, jumping fences and logs and even haystacks just for the fun of it. His father would have killed him if he'd known, but John hadn't been able to resist, especially since it had been so clear that the mare enjoyed the game as much as he did.

Yes, Liberty could clear four feet. The question was, did she have enough energy remaining in her to do it now?

John didn't know. But he could see no other option. All he could do was try—and count on his mare's tremendous heart to save them both.

One more glance back showed that the redcoats were growing ever closer. The lead rider was grinning as he urged his sweaty horse on faster. Even at a distance of seven or eight lengths, John could see the glitter of victory in the man's eyes.

Returning his gaze forward, John took a deep breath, trying not to think too hard about what he was about to do. Then he pulled Liberty sharply off to the right.

She tossed her head, caught by surprise. But she veered off the road as directed, slowing slightly in the softer footing of the grassy verge. Her ears pricked forward as she spotted the wall just a few strides ahead.

"Come on, girl!" John shouted, clamping his legs against her sides. "You can do it!"

Liberty's gallop steadied and slowed slightly. One stride out, John felt her rock back and balance herself. He smiled. He knew she wouldn't let him down. . . .

"Hey! Stop, boy!" the soldiers yelled from somewhere behind him.

But John hardly heard them. Time seemed to slow down as he felt his horse's powerful haunches gather beneath him. Her forelegs lifted, and those hindquarters propelled her forward and upward, launching her over the wall.

Even so, she barely managed to clear it. One of her front hooves struck the top of the wall, sending a couple of rocks flying. She lurched downward again, twisting her hindquarters to one side to avoid scraping them on the wall, and landed hard with a loud grunt, her head flying down for balance until her nose nearly touched the ground.

John had stayed centered over the horse in the air, but the hard landing and twist to the side knocked him off balance. He pitched forward, grabbing for mane as he found himself staring down at the mare's withers. For a moment he thought he would be able to shove himself back into the saddle again.

But then Liberty stumbled, unable to control her forward momentum after the hard landing. Her forelegs flailed as she tried desperately to keep from going down on her knees.

She managed, just barely, but that last lurch was too much for John. He felt himself flying forward over her head, flipping over completely before hitting the rocky ground, one leg crumpled beneath him.

Ten

"Aargh!" John shouted at the top of his lungs as fire shot up through his left leg. He knew at once that he was badly hurt.

Clutching his injured leg and biting hard on his lower lip to try to distract himself from the pain, he rolled into a sitting position. His vision blurred and he swayed under a new wave of pain. But when the black spots faded, he was relieved to see Liberty prancing and snorting nearby. She appeared unhurt aside from a scrape on her front fetlock. Tossing her head, she trotted over and skidded to a stop in front of him, lowering her head as if wondering what he was doing on the ground.

With a groan, John grabbed the mare's closest leg and hauled himself to his feet. But as soon as he put weight on his left leg he screamed in agony and nearly collapsed again; blackness swirled once more around the edges of his mind, threatening to overtake him.

There was a shout from nearby. Shaking his head to

clear it, John glanced over and saw several redcoats peering over the wall from atop their horses.

"Come on, men!" one of them yelled. "He's down—let's go get him!"

That made John forget the pain in his leg for the moment. Grabbing the saddle with one hand and Liberty's mane with the other, he hauled himself up onto her back, for once grateful that she wasn't taller. He almost passed out again when he flung his right leg over to the proper side, causing his injured left leg to bang against the saddle.

But by the time several of his pursuers had scrambled over the wall and started running toward him on foot, he'd gotten himself into some semblance of a riding position. Leaving his stirrups to flap empty against the horse's sides, he clucked to Liberty and turned her away from the soldiers. She responded immediately, breaking into a trot for a few excruciating strides before settling into the much smoother canter.

John clung to the cantle, willing himself to remain conscious. All he had to do was reach Waltham. . . .

"I still don't know how you did it, John." Alice leaned

down and pressed a cool, damp rag against her brother's forehead, her brow knitted with concern. "Duncan told me that when you reached the meeting spot in Waltham, they did not know if you would make it."

"I don't remember that much about the ride," John admitted, his voice sounding raspy and tired. "And I don't really remember anything after getting to Waltham. Perhaps that is for the best. George tells me he carried me across the front of the saddle while Duncan ponied Liberty behind." He closed his eyes for a moment, drained of energy just from those few words. "That horse saved my life," he added weakly. "Is she okay? Is someone taking care of her? If she'd run away when I came off, or tried any of her usual antics after that . . ."

"Hush. She's just fine." Alice brushed back his damp hair. "You're safe now, and that's all that matters. And Dr. Goodwin says your leg will be good as new after six weeks of care—it was a clean break."

John glanced down at his leg, to which the local doctor had applied a splint and a cast of wax and cloth. The pain had mostly receded to a dull throb, though it increased alarmingly with any attempt at movement.

At that moment their father strode into the room, followed by the twins. "Awake then, are we, son?" he asked gruffly. "Good. Then perhaps you can explain to me why you were off messing about and getting yourself hurt when there's so much work to do here?"

John felt a flash of irritation. He was tempted to retort that Thomas was the one who had spent much of his life "messing about" in his fruitless treasure hunts, leaving John extra work at home.

But he bit his tongue. Alice had already told him how anxious their father had been when he'd heard John was hurt. This was merely his clumsy way of showing it.

"I am sorry, Father," he said. "The doctor said I'll be able to hobble around a bit within a week or two. At least then I'll be able to help with the harness and such."

Humility yanked at his bedsheet to straighten it. "He can shell the beans, too, Father," she suggested hopefully. "His hands still work, do they not? I can even bring them upstairs to him if you like."

John made a face at her. Shelling beans was a task left to the twins, and one they particularly hated.

"All right then," Thomas said gruffly. "Now that I see

you're awake, I'd best get back to work. Someone needs to pay the bills." He turned and stalked out of the room without another word.

Mercy rolled her eyes dramatically. "Look what you've done, John," she complained. "Father has been in a terrible mood since you got hurt."

Mercy was saved from John's angry retort by the sound of footsteps on the landing outside. "May we come in?" George's familiar voice called.

Immediately John's mood brightened. He had not seen his friends since they'd brought him home.

"Come in!" he called. "My sisters were just leaving." He shot a pointed look at both twins.

Alice put a hand on Mercy's back and steered her toward the door. "Yes, we'll leave you alone," she said. "Come, Humility. I believe Elizabeth left you a lovely pile of beans to be shelled."

George and Duncan burst in just as the girls reached the door, nearly causing a collision. "Oh!" Duncan said, stopping so quickly that his cane squeaked against the floorboards. His cheeks went pink. "Begging your pardon, Miss Alice. I should have been more cautious."

"No pardon needed," Alice replied with a smile. "It was entirely our fault."

"Stop begging pardons and get over here," John called impatiently. In his waking moments since returning home, he'd been distracting himself from the pain in his leg by thinking about the clue they'd found in Dorchester, and he longed to discuss it. He wished Alice could stay, too. But she was already bustling out with the twins.

"How is the leg, my friend?" George asked, glancing at the cast, which rested above the bedclothes.

"The right one has never felt better," John joked, wriggling the foot of his uninjured leg.

George chuckled, but Duncan's expression remained somber. "I wish to thank you, John," he said. "If you had not led those lobsterbacks away . . ."

"Never mind." John shook his head, refusing to let him finish. "I only did what was necessary."

"Nevertheless, I shall not forget it." Duncan bit his lip, staring at John's broken leg.

"Let's just hope the trip to Dorchester will prove worth all the trouble," George put in, pulling a bit of paper out of his clothes. "I took the liberty of retrieving this from your saddlebags, and Duncan and I have been pondering it ever since." He shook his head. "But to no avail, I'm afraid."

"I have been thinking about it, too. I still wonder if it might refer to a choir or perhaps the lyric to a song." John sighed in frustration, glancing down at his bad leg. "I only wish I were not stuck in bed! You two shall have to continue the quest without me for a while—I'm afraid we dare not wait for my leg to heal. If all those lobsterbacks are any indication, England is growing worried."

George nodded. "It would help us greatly if we knew what it is we are seeking," he complained. "It sounds as if your Mr. Revere was not very clear on that matter."

"I wonder if perhaps the treasure could be a lot of valuables—gold and jewels and such—that could then be used to hire mercenaries or bribe loyalists or purchase munitions . . ." John shrugged. "In any case, we know that whatever it is, it's important to the Patriot cause. And that is reason enough to keep searching."

"Good morning, son. Is Thomas Gates here?"

John glanced up. He'd been so engrossed in restitching a leather browband that he hadn't heard the harness shop's door open. Now he saw a tall, lean young stranger standing before him.

"My father is not home at the moment," John said, shifting his weight carefully to avoid jostling his bad leg. "Can I help you with something?"

Nearly two weeks had passed since his accident, and he was able to hobble about now with the aid of a pair of canes. Over a week in bed had left him too restless to do otherwise.

"My name is Cooper," the stranger said. "I'm here from Lexington. Your father had a breastplate of mine in for repair."

"Let me see if I can find it." John pushed himself upright and hobbled over to the pile of finished pieces awaiting delivery or pickup.

Cooper glanced curiously at John's splinted leg but didn't ask about it. Instead, he glanced out the open door. "The temperature has fallen fast this week, has it not?"

"Indeed," John agreed. "I am afraid it might be a hard winter."

"I share your fear," Cooper said with a short laugh. "Though I wish it were due only to the weather. If the

Continental Congress cannot find a solution to the problems with the king, I fear it could be a very hard winter indeed—for all of us."

"Ah, you are a Patriot, then?" John asked, a bit warily. If Cooper were a Loyalist, John did not want to betray his true feelings. On the other hand, in his current state it was difficult to keep up on what was happening in the larger world and he was eager for word. He had had to rely on the few nuggets of information Alice picked up in the town square or at the tavern, along with infrequent visits from George and Duncan, for the latest news. Until finding himself confined to his bed, John hadn't realized just how involved he'd begun to feel in the Patriot cause.

"Yes, I am a member of the Lexington militia," Cooper replied proudly. "Part of our Minuteman unit, standing ready to repel the Tory threat whenever needed."

"My friend George is a Minuteman here in Concord," John said as he continued sifting through various bits of tack. "He was telling me yesterday that the Suffolk Resolves denouncing the Intolerable Acts have just been adopted by the Continental Congress currently convened in Philadelphia. . . ."

The two of them chatted about that and other political matters until John finally located the breastplate. Then he handed it over, naming the usual price for such a repair.

At that, Cooper hesitated. "Er—your father told me it would not be necessary to pay the full sum." He handed over an amount equaling less than half the figure John had named.

John stared at the money in confusion. But before he could respond, his father bustled into the shop. Spotting Cooper immediately, Thomas hurried over and clapped him on the shoulder.

"Hello again, my young friend," he said. "I think you'll find your breastplate good as new, eh?" Seeing the money in John's hand, he took it from him and pressed it back on the Minuteman. "And your money is no good here. Be off with you now—and take care of yourself."

"Thank you kindly, Mr. Gates," Cooper said with a tip of his hat. "You are a good man."

As the militiaman left, John stared at his father in confusion. It wasn't like Thomas to give a stranger something for nothing. And now, especially, he could ill afford such generosity, as the entire family was feeling the loss of John's post-rider income during his recuperation.

"Why didn't you let him pay?" he blurted out as Thomas stepped over to grab a freshly mended saddle off its rack. "We need the money."

Thomas shot him an unreadable glance. "Indeed we do," he said. "But some matters are of more importance than money, my boy."

Before John could say anything else, Thomas turned and hurried out of the shop carrying the saddle. John stared after him.

And all this time I've thought the old man disinterested in politics, even neutral, he mused. *Perhaps he is more Patriot than I had ever realized.*

The next few weeks passed slowly. But John's leg was healing, and before long he was able to get around well enough to help his sisters with many of the household tasks and even do some of the stable chores. Finally, the doctor removed his cast, though he warned John to be easy on it for a while and not to try to ride again for at least another week. John grudgingly agreed and tried to busy himself with other tasks.

One chilly afternoon at the end of October, John was helping Alice carry wood inside for the fire. As they worked, the discussion turned to the Dorchester clue. While Alice had seen it on several occasions, she had no more idea than the boys about what it might mean.

"Could the verse be guiding us to a particular song-book?" she wondered, dumping her armful of kindling near the hearth and brushing off her hands on her skirts. "You know, as in the bit about 'our voices blend in song.' Perhaps another clue is written within such a book?"

John dropped his own load of split logs. "Perhaps. But then what of the lines about kin and independent mind and so forth?" He sighed loudly, feeling frustration bubble up within him. He simply could not puzzle out this latest riddle. "I am beginning to wonder if the hunt will go no further than this clue. If I can't decipher it, then the trust Alden put in me will have been for naught. Perhaps I should have gone back to Mr. Hale . . ."

"Stop speaking that way," Alice interrupted. "Can this quest of yours make much difference? Maybe you *should* stop fretting over it so much and leave it to those clever men who are meeting down in Philadelphia."

"The Congress has just ended this week," John said automatically. "George mentioned it yesterday." But he wasn't really thinking about that. His brow furrowed.

"What is it, John?" Alice asked, noticing his expression.

"Philadelphia," John repeated slowly. Then he gasped. "Philadelphia! That's it!"

Eleven

"What, no Liberty mare for you this time?" George asked when John led a trio of horses out of the stable two weeks later.

John grimaced. "I promised Father I would take an easier mount for my first long ride now that I've healed," he admitted, busying himself with tightening the girth of Duncan's horse. "He thinks I am merely taking a leisurely trip to Watertown with a few letters, so I do not dare do anything to arouse his suspicions."

A few minutes later, they set off on the latest leg of their hunt. December was just around the corner by now, the wind had an icy bite to it, and a dusting of fresh snow coated the fields and roads.

For a while they rode in silence, each lost in his own thoughts. John found his mind wandering back over the clues that had led them to this moment and he recited it under his breath.

We are eight strong
Our voices blend in song
If ye wish our secret free
Our Kin's verse holds the Key
Be of Independent mind
Out from our door direction find.

Alice's mention of Philadelphia had brought to mind the capitalized word "Independent" in the clue. Based on the other clues that made use of capitalization, John suspected that it might not refer to the word but to a thing—like the Old State House Bell in Philadelphia, which was also commonly known as the "Independence Bell." Sharing this with George and Duncan had then led to the idea that the line "voices blend in song" could indicate another bell or group of bells such as the eight atop Christ Church in Boston.

The trio had gotten stuck again for a little while after that, not certain what the rest of the clue might mean. But further contemplation had presented the idea that the "kin's verse" that held the key might reference the Bible verse inscribed on the Independence Bell. Something John's sister,

Elizabeth, had helped with. Overhearing the boys discussing the bell in the tavern, she had asked:

"Ah, are you talking of the State House Bell in Philadelphia?" Elizabeth's smile had widened, and she'd clasped her hands before her as if in prayer. "*Proclaim liberty throughout all the land unto all the inhabitants thereof.*"

All three boys had stared at her, perplexed. "Huh?" George had responded for all of them.

Elizabeth had tsk-tsked. "Do you three never read your Bibles, nor stay awake at church?" she chided gently. "Our preacher mentioned once in his sermon that those words are inscribed on the bell. I know it by heart—it is Leviticus 25:10."

The boys still hadn't been certain what the Bible verse might mean. But knowing that an inscription was indeed on the bell had made them confident enough to head to Boston. If there was an inscription on one of the bells mentioned in the clue, perhaps there would be a significant inscription on the other bells mentioned. They would take a look around Christ Church with the verse in mind and see what they found.

However, they hadn't been able to set off for nearly two weeks. John's leg was still weak, George had his usual

Minuteman duties to attend to, and Duncan's father was being more possessive than ever of his time.

Finally, though, the day had come when John's leg felt strong enough and George had a few days off. Luckily, this coincided with a journey by Duncan's parents to visit relatives for the week up in Andover, and Duncan was able to get out of the trip by feigning a slight fever.

"We shall just have to go to the church and take a look around," John said now, shifting in the saddle to favor his newly healed leg. "It worked for us in Dorchester. Maybe we shall be lucky again."

But upon arriving, they once again found their plans thwarted. After making their way across the city, they finally came within sight of Christ Church, only to find dozens of uniformed soldiers gathered in the square before it, practicing formations and marching about. The three friends quickly ducked around the corner of the nearest building.

"They cannot march around here forever, right?" John asked. "We shall just have to wait them out."

And wait they did. After stowing their horses at a nearby stable, they hid themselves in a deep doorway where the marching soldiers would not easily spy them, but from which they had a clear view of square and church. An hour passed, then two more. The wind was blowing hard and cold off the harbor, the frigid air seeped through their clothes, and the forced stillness caused John's bad leg to ache. They dared converse only in whispers, and soon settled into silence, watching the redcoats march to and fro without comment.

Eventually John grew so bored that he resorted to counting the bricks in the church building's grand facade. In doing so, he hit upon an idea.

"What if the clue isn't in the bells *or* the words of the Bible verse, but rather its *designation*?" he suggested. "Elizabeth said it was Leviticus 25:10. We could be meant to count twenty-five bricks up from the ground, then ten over from the corner, or some such."

"No!" Duncan exclaimed, smacking his forehead with eyes wide and excited. "If indeed it's bricks we're meant to count, we need to count over from the *door*! Remember that final line? 'Out from our door direction find.' That's it!"

George shook his head, looking confused. "But how do you know we are meant to count bricks and not paces or city blocks or anything else?"

"We don't," John said with a shrug. "But it's as good a theory to start with as any, don't you think? In any case, I suppose it is provident that we have been forced to wait here. Had we not sat staring at the church for hours on end, we might have searched the whole place through without figuring out that we were meant to use the numbers of the verse in that way." Now that he had hit upon that idea, he felt confident that it was correct, whether indicating bricks or paces.

It wasn't until the last daylight had faded and the moon had risen overhead that the soldiers started drifting away and not returning. Finally there was not a red coat or a musket left in sight. Even then, Duncan insisted they wait a while more to be certain the regulars wouldn't suddenly return.

But at last the three friends made their way over to the front of the church. "All right," John said, keeping his voice hushed to avoid attracting attention from nearby houses. "Let's try this counting-bricks thing. . . ."

He stepped to the right side of the door frame and began counting carefully outward—as the clue had suggested. When he reached the twenty-fifth brick, he kept one hand on it while counting ten bricks up from the ground.

"That should be it," whispered Duncan, who was watching carefully. "Is there anything written on it, or is it loose perhaps?"

The moonlight was bright enough so they could see easily, and John could make out no difference between the brick and its neighbors. He pushed it, but it seemed firm in its place.

"No good?" George said. "Let's try counting ten out and twenty-five up instead. Perhaps that's the one we want. Or perhaps we should try counting paces instead of bricks for a while?" He glanced around. "Either way, we must hurry! There's no telling if the king's men might return."

"Why don't you keep a lookout just in case?" John said.

George nodded and strode across the square to a spot with a vantage down the street in each direction. Meanwhile Duncan started counting as John stepped back, puzzling over what they knew. It seemed odd that the numbers of the verses should be reversed as George suggested—had they missed something? Or would they have to attempt every permutation of the Leviticus verse in every direction and from every door. . . .

Suddenly he gasped. "No, wait!" he said. "I know what we're doing wrong. We are meant to count out to the left, not the right—*L* for left, *L* for Leviticus!"

"Brilliant!" Duncan exclaimed, immediately abandoning his counting and hurrying over to the other side of the door. "Now, let's see—one, two—"

"Away!" George hissed, running toward them from his lookout spot. "The regulars are on their way back, and they're almost upon us!"

Twelve

George and Duncan instantly scurried off in the direction of their earlier hiding spot. But John hesitated, unable to bear the thought of more hours huddled in that cold doorway staring helplessly at the church. He could hear the sounds of voices and laughter approaching from down the street, but the redcoats were not yet in sight. Perhaps there was still enough time . . .

"John! What are you doing?" Duncan called softly from halfway across the square, where he'd paused to look back.

John ignored him, counting bricks as quickly as he could. Twenty-five out, ten up . . .

"Got it!" he murmured as his fingers touched the rough, cool surface of what he thought was the correct brick. Once again it appeared blank and unsullied at first glance. But when he pushed at it, it moved slightly!

"Are you insane?" George had just rushed back to where John was standing. He grabbed his arm. "We have to go—they'll be here any second!"

"I found it!" John shook off George's grip, wedging his fingers into the indent of mortar around the brick, trying to jiggle it loose. But his fingers were too big to get much of a purchase.

"Let me try."

John realized that Duncan had returned to his side as well. He gulped and glanced over his shoulder toward the street, hoping he hadn't just doomed his friends.

But Duncan's nimble fingers were already working at the brick. John held his breath, watching. Within seconds, the brick popped out of place. Duncan stuck his hand into the hole it left and pulled out a small wooden box.

"Got it!" he whispered.

George grabbed the brick, which had tumbled to the ground, and jammed it back in place. "Come on!" he hissed. Grabbing Duncan unceremoniously around the waist, he hoisted him to one shoulder like a sack of wheat and took off at a run.

John was right behind them. They skidded into their hiding place just as the first of the king's men rounded the corner into the square.

"Whew!" John collapsed against the wall. "That was close."

He peered out to see what was happening—and was startled to see one of the redcoats peering back in his direction! The soldier let out a shout, and several others hurried toward him. With a gulp, John pulled back quickly.

"Er, perhaps *too* close," he told his friends. "I think they've spotted us!"

Not waiting to see if John was right, they jumped out of the doorway and took off in the other direction. This time George left Duncan on his own two feet, though he and John were both careful not to leave him behind as they slipped and skidded down the icy cobblestoned streets. John had often thought that the streets of Boston resembled a maze, and for once he was glad of that. After a few twists and turns, their pursuers had fallen well behind.

"This way!" John hissed, gesturing to his friends. He led them into the old Copp's Hill burial ground, where they quickly found hiding spots behind a few of the larger grave markers. Crouching down, they waited to see if the redcoats would find them there. But before long the shouts seemed to come from farther away rather than closer. A short time later, the shouts faded altogether and the only sound to be heard was the labored breathing of the three boys.

"I think we lost them," George whispered when the silence continued.

"I suppose they're not likely to try very hard to find us," Duncan pointed out, leaning on his cane. "For all they know, we were just curious kids hanging about."

George nodded. "True. But I'll feel better when we've put even more distance between us and them."

John had to agree with that. "Do you still have the box?" he asked Duncan. At his friend's nod, he added, "Then let's leave the horses where they are for the night and head down to my cousin's house. We can take a look at it once we're safely there."

The cold night air and the adrenaline from the chase lent extra speed to their feet, and soon the three friends were rounding the corner onto King Street, where John's cousin lived. George was in the lead at the time, and he stopped short, causing Duncan to bump into him and let out a soft oath.

"Hush!" George hissed, stepping quickly backward and pushing the other two with him.

"What is it?" John asked, thinking only of getting inside so that his cousin's wife could fix them a warm drink.

In answer, George merely pointed. John stepped forward and peered around the corner. Then he gasped, all thoughts of warm drinks forgotten.

"Lobsterbacks!" he whispered in disbelief, staring at the two soldiers standing on the doorstep laughing and chatting with his cousin. Could it be? Had his cousins gone to the Loyalist side?

Duncan had come forward to look, too. "Now what?" he whispered. "Do you think your relative is truly a Tory? Or is he merely acting the part to avoid trouble from the lobsterbacks?"

"I do not know. But we can't take any chances," John said grimly. "We cannot stay here tonight after all. If only we knew where Mr. Revere's home was located, I'm sure he'd take us in. . . ."

"Oh, but I do know," Duncan said. "He lives at number 19 North-Square." At John's surprised look, he smiled and added, "I saw it written on some papers when we visited his shop some weeks back."

Sending up a silent prayer of thanks for his friend's

sharp eyesight and good memory, John turned away without a backward glance at his cousin. "Come," he said, "let's get ourselves to North-Square then."

Before long they were knocking tentatively at the door of a large, handsome home with a steeply pitched roof, grayish-taupe siding, and diamond-paned casement windows. There was a long delay before they finally heard the sound of shuffling footsteps on the other side of the door. At last the door swung open, and Paul Revere looked out at them with sleepy eyes.

"Our apologies for disturbing you so late, sir," John said. "We have been having some troubles with the regulars tonight, and . . ."

Revere was already looking more alert. "Come in," he said. "Quickly. It is no trouble at all—I am glad you came."

Soon the three friends were warming themselves beside the fire in a large, comfortable parlor framed with heavy wooden beams. John introduced George, who had not met the silversmith before. Then all three of them took turns relating their adventures of that day and night. Revere, his eyes wide, listened with great interest.

"The Linonians have certainly done their best to ensure that only a Patriot would ever be able to solve their clues," he commented when John mentioned the many clues they had uncovered. "I only hope they have not made things so difficult that it shall be impossible to find what they have hidden in time!"

With a jolt, John realized they hadn't yet so much as glanced inside the box they'd found in the church wall. Duncan seemed to be thinking along the same lines, for at that moment he pulled it out of his jacket.

"Shall we see what we have this time?" he suggested. "Perhaps with Mr. Revere's help we can solve the next puzzle that most likely awaits."

John glanced uncertainly at Revere. The silversmith's earlier reluctance to get directly involved with the clues was fresh in his mind. But this time Revere hesitated only briefly before nodding.

"All right," Revere said. "I suppose it wouldn't do any harm for me to see what you've found."

Duncan opened the box. Once again, it held only a slip of paper. This time, in addition to a brief verse, the paper contained a series of Roman numerals and ordinary numbers.

We have been unfairly Stamped by royal decree.
A cipher true to thee and me!
VII-2; XIII-19; XI-9; XII-4; IX-5; IV-21; II-23;
X-12; I-27; V-14; VII-14; III-3; VI-6

"Not another cipher!" George exclaimed in dismay.

"It appears so," John said. "Those pairs of numbers must hold the key."

"Indeed." Revere was staring at the paper, stroking his chin with a thoughtful expression. "In fact, it reminds me of a fellow of my acquaintance—an agitator by the name of Mr. Benedict Arnold. A good Patriot man, and very clever. I once spent an evening drinking with him in a Boston tavern, and Arnold spent much of that evening showing off some parlor tricks involving the making of codes out of certain words within the Bible and such as that. Those numbers could very well be verses from the Bible."

John brightened immediately, recalling the importance of the Bible verse number on the Independence Bell in the previous clue. "That must be how we solve *this* clue! Perhaps it was written by the same individual," he said.

"We should be able to decode it with little trouble."

"May we borrow a Bible?" Duncan asked Revere eagerly.

He nodded, pointing across the room at a thick leather-bound book resting on a table near the window. "It is over there."

John took a step toward it, but at that moment a woman bustled into the room wearing a bedgown over her shift. She was slender and kind-eyed, with masses of dark hair that drifted down over her narrow shoulders and threatened to come completely unpinned.

"Oh dear, what is all the commotion down here?" she asked, taking in the sight of the three boys. "Paul, have you brought guests in without alerting me?"

"I'm afraid so, Rachel, my dear," Revere admitted with an indulgent smile. "My young friends are visiting from Concord and have found themselves stranded in Boston without lodging."

"Oh, my." Rachel tut-tutted sympathetically. "And on such a cold night! Come now, boys. Let's get you warmed up and comfortable. . . ."

John glanced helplessly at the leather-bound Bible just a

few steps away. But Revere seemed quite willing to let his wife do as she pleased, and so there was little John and his friends could do but go along with her as she herded them off to bed.

Thirteen

"What do you think, boys?" John asked quietly, leaning forward on the dining table to speak to his friends. "Should we ride for home right away or stay here until we solve the clue?"

Duncan glanced over toward the fire before answering. Paul Revere had left for his shop a few minutes earlier, but his wife, Rachel, his teenage daughter, Deborah, and two younger daughters were still in the kitchen cleaning up the breakfast things and periodically checking on the baby sleeping in a cradle near the fire. Revere's son and a couple of younger daughters had run off after eating and were nowhere to be seen.

"I think we ought to stay," Duncan murmured. "Why waste time? For all we know the clue could direct us to another spot in Boston."

George looked worried. "But it is a long ride home," he said. "We shouldn't stay away too long."

John shot him a sympathetic look, guessing that he was feeling guilty about being so far from his fellow Minutemen. "This Bible cipher shouldn't take long," John said by way of answer. "We'll stay and solve it here, then decide what we do from there."

After thanking the Revere women for the meal, the three friends repaired to the parlor. They retrieved the Bible from its table and set to work trying to solve the clue.

But they had no luck. Matching the numbers given with Bible verses turned out only gibberish. After a while, George threw up his hands in frustration.

"You said this wouldn't take long," he told John. "But at this rate, we could be in Boston through spring!"

Duncan was staring at the clue. "I have a thought," he said. "We have paid little mind to those lines above the numbers. What if they are somehow meant to indicate which book within the Bible we are supposed to use?"

John glanced at the lines. "*We have been unfairly Stamped by royal decree . . .*" he read aloud. Suddenly the answer struck him. "Oh!" he cried, once again dumbfounded that he could have missed something so obvious for so long. "We *have* been going about this all wrong!"

"I knew it," George said. "Wait, what?"

John stabbed one finger at the lines. "We were never meant to look in the Bible at all," he said. "We only got that idea in our heads because of what Mr. Revere said last night and the previous clue. But in fact, there is no mention of the Bible at all. And the true meaning is in fact rather obvious—it is the detestable Stamp Act that is meant to be our key!"

"Oh!" Comprehension dawned on Duncan's face, though George still appeared a bit confused. "That does make sense. It is another riddle meant for a Patriot—for a Patriot would be most likely to remember the outrage of the Stamp Act, even though it happened nearly ten years ago and has long been repealed." He shrugged. "But this makes our task more difficult. Where shall we find a copy of the Stamp Act?"

"I have an idea about that. . . ."

A few minutes later the three of them were in Revere's silver shop explaining their mission. It was quiet within the shop; only two workers toiled in the back, and though the boys passed a departing customer on their way in, there were no others to be seen inside.

"Hmm," Revere said after he'd heard them out. He rubbed his chin and glanced around the shop. "You could just be correct about that. Let me see if I have a copy of the detestable act somewhere."

He spent the next few minutes shuffling through papers. Finally he found a rather battered copy of the Stamp Act and handed it over.

"You may work over there if you like," he said, pointing toward an unused table at one side of the shop. "Let me know how you make out."

John smiled when he glanced at the act, which was divided into sections headed by Roman numerals. "Perfect," he said as he and his friends hurried over to the table Revere had indicated. "It looks as if we need to find the numbered heading and then count in a certain number of words to find the right one. See? The first pair of numbers is VII-2. If we look under the heading VII, we find that the second word is, um . . ." He paused, locating the right spot on the page. "It is the word 'always,'" he continued. "If we go on like that, surely the words will spell out some kind of message or direction."

They set to work. George read out each pair of

numbers, then John would count to the indicated word and read it aloud while Duncan would write it down on a separate piece of paper. However, once again it seemed not to work as they had hoped. In the end they came up with only another nonsensical phrase:

ALWAYS THE SHALL FURTHER IN WRITING CONTRACTED
PROCLAMATION REPLICATION PAMPHLETS OF IT SHALL

John bit his lip, staring at the meaningless lines.

"Doesn't make much sense," George commented.

"Never mind," Duncan said. "We must still be missing something. Perhaps we are meant to shift the order of the words, or use only the initial letters, or count backward instead of forward, or otherwise decipher it further." He shrugged. "After all, it is just too logical that the creators of this trail would use the Stamp Act in such a simple way. We cannot give up yet."

John nodded his agreement. His friend was right. The answer had to lie in the Stamp Act; as they'd said earlier, the hated act had bonded every Patriot at the time. Like the recent Intolerable Acts, it had brought them together against a common enemy, even causing them to convene a special congress in New York.

"Wait," he said slowly. "I just thought of something. We're working with the original Stamp Act; the unjust proclamation handed down by the king. But perhaps what we really need is to consider the *Patriot* side of things." A smile broke over his face as his mind cleared, and he knew he'd found the right answer. "We need to try again. But this time we need to use the text written in *response* to the Act by the Stamp Act Congress right here in the colonies!"

Luckily Revere had a copy of that document as well. Like its predecessor, it consisted primarily of a list of clauses sectioned off with Roman numerals. This time Duncan offered to count out each word, and John took the quill from him to write down the results.

As he waited between words, he found himself wondering what his father would say if he could see him now. After all, if not for all those childhood lessons and discussions on treasure hunting, it seemed unlikely that John would have been able to come this far on his quest. When was it that he had started to think his father's interests foolish, anyway? Was it something that had come to him from his own mind and opinions, or had he merely listened too much to what other people thought? Perhaps when he and his friends found this treasure, it would offer a chance to quiet all those naysayers and wags who liked to claim that Thomas Gates had wasted his life in pursuit of hopeless dreams, just as his father's father had done before him. Perhaps it would even offer a way to recapture the easy bond that John and his father had once shared.

Time passed swiftly with such thoughts and with the task at hand. Before long the trio had a new version of the clue:

> The house of Prosperity by commons within center realm therein subject is crown.

"Hmm." Duncan drummed his slender fingers on the tabletop. "That doesn't make much more sense than the first one."

But John was convinced they had it right this time and said as much. "This one has to be correct," he said. "It simply *feels* correct. I suspect we have only to figure out what it is telling us."

Duncan nodded agreeably. "All right," he said. "House

of Prosperity—that could mean a wealthy man's home, could it not? Or perhaps a private bank." He glanced around at the silver items gleaming out from shelves and tabletops all around them. "Or even a shop filled with valuable items such as this one."

"Indeed," John said. "If we can figure out how to tie that phrase together with the rest, perhaps it will become more clear."

"Well, one thing *is* clear," George said, sounding rather impatient. "We do not know what this is about—as usual. And if things go as usual from here, it could be weeks before we work it out. Therefore I see no reason we cannot continue this discussion on horseback as we ride for home."

John and Duncan exchanged a glance. It was obvious that George was growing impatient about leaving his militia for so long.

"All right," John said reluctantly. "Let's just tell Mr. Revere what we've discovered. Then we shall go and retrieve the horses."

When John led his horse into the stable at home, weary after the long ride home from Boston, he was shocked to find a pair of British Regulars lounging just inside with their coats unbuttoned and their feet up on one of the hitching rails. For a moment his heart raced and he was tempted to leap back into the saddle and gallop away. Had the king's men somehow found out what he'd been up to or heard of his recent adventures from those redcoats they'd escaped in Boston?

But at that moment his sister Elizabeth entered behind him carrying a pitcher of beer. "Oh! John, you have returned," she said. "Have you met our—er, guests—yet?"

It was not often that Elizabeth's voice revealed anything but her usual sunny, pleasant outlook on life. But now John detected a definite touch of disdain as she glanced at the two men.

"Er . . ." he began, still not certain what was going on.

"Brought us something to drink at last, have you?" one of the soldiers called out with a guffaw. He was a tall man, built like a rough-cut pine plank, with hair the shade of a wild stag's coat and very pale blue eyes. "Send t'other one out next time, will you, lass? The pretty young bird with the dark hair."

John's fists clenched at his sides as he realized the man

was referring to Alice. "I beg your pardon?" he began hotly. "I'll thank you not to—"

"John! Come with me." Elizabeth set down the pitcher and grabbed his arm. With uncharacteristic firmness, she dragged him back outside with his horse trailing along behind them at the end of its reins.

"What's going on here?" he demanded, shaking his arm free so vigorously that the horse let out a snort of alarm. "What are those two lobsterbacks doing in there, messing up our stable?"

"It is the Quartering Act." Elizabeth's face was grim. "A regiment of regulars has chosen to take up residence in this neighborhood, and several of their number are staying within our stable. They arrived only a few hours after you rode off for Boston the other morning." She glanced toward the soldiers, who were visible within the stable aisle busying themselves with the beer she'd brought. "What's more, it seems that loutish, arrogant, loudmouthed fellow has taken a fancy to Alice. Frederick, I believe he is called."

John was shocked, partly because he'd never heard Elizabeth use such uncharitable language to describe another human being, and partly due to the meaning behind those words. "The Quartering Act . . ." he repeated dumbly.

"Do not make trouble, John, please," Elizabeth begged. "I know they are insufferable. But it is the law; we have to let them stay. What else can we do? Besides, if you defy them or make them angry, they will only throw you in the stocks, and perhaps Father with you. That is, if they do not decide to have you drawn and quartered, or burn down the stable as I hear they've done in other villages . . ." She broke off in a sob. "Please, John. Say you will not antagonize them while they are here."

John took a deep breath, knowing she was right but almost—*almost*—being angry enough not to care.

"John?" Elizabeth prompted anxiously.

"I shall try," he muttered at last through great effort of will. "But I cannot make any promises."

Over the next couple of weeks, the regulars made themselves more and more at home in the Gates family's livery stable, creating themselves bunks in the stalls and tack room and forcing John's sisters to fetch them food and drink at all hours of the day. It was not an easy thing for John to witness in passive silence, especially whenever he heard the revolting Frederick howling for Alice. He generally found it easier to stay away from home as much as possible, taking care of necessary stable chores early in the morning while the resident redcoats were still sleeping off the effects of John's father's best rum and whiskey and returning only as necessary to take care of the occasional post ride or other business.

The rest of the time, John distracted himself as best he could by discussing the latest clue with his friends. After some time, they had puzzled out that "commons" could refer to Boston Common and immediately chastised themselves for not figuring that out while in Boston.

With little desire to stay in regular-occupied Concord, it was decided that they would make the trip back to Boston as soon as possible. But fate seemed against them, and they were not able to get away until a couple of days before Christmas. Even then, Duncan was not able to come with John and George. His family insisted he remain at home with them to receive some relatives visiting from New Hampshire.

Fortunately, neither John's family, nor George's, was

much interested in Christmas, that holiday being rather too English in nature for their current tastes. And so the two of them set off one fine, cold December morning on yet another journey into Boston.

Fourteen

John spent much of the long ride to Boston hoping that all would become clear once they saw the Common. But when he and George reached it and looked out over its snow-coated expanse, they found neither answers nor ideas forthcoming.

"What now?" George asked.

John bit his lip. "I do not know," he admitted. "Perhaps we should go speak with Mr. Revere. He might have an idea for us."

When they reached the silversmith's shop, they found him entertaining several visitors. John immediately recognized one of them as John Hancock, whom he'd encountered in that very shop more than a year ago. Revere soon introduced the others. One was a sharp-gazed young man named Samuel Osgood, and another Osgood's cousin Charles, a fresh-faced fellow just a few years older than John and George.

"And finally, of course, we have Mr. Samuel Adams, recently returned from the Continental Congress in Philadelphia," Revere finished, gesturing toward the final member of the group, a distinguished-looking gray-haired man in his fifties. "Adams, I'm pleased to present my young Patriot friends Mr. Gates and Mr. Chase."

John gulped. Adams had to be one of the most famous men in Boston—possibly in all the colonies.

"A pleasure to meet you all," George said, shaking hands with each of the men. "Our apologies for interrupting."

Revere put a hand on his shoulder. "No need to apologize," he said. "We always welcome an interruption from one of our brave young Minutemen."

"In any case, we were discussing the current situation in the outlying villages," Samuel Osgood said. "I have just arrived from Andover and asked my cousin to introduce me to these fine gentlemen, as I am becoming increasingly concerned about the behavior of local Loyalists. It almost seems that they do not care how much are liberties are trampled upon."

"Indeed," Adams said gravely, his lined face shadowy in the shop's dim lighting. "Some might argue that we should try to find common ground with our adversaries. However, it seems that the king's men—including the Loyalists and the king himself—are willing to make no compromise. They call our response sedition, but what else are we to do when Parliament shows no respect for our rights? Why should we remain yoked to a fading and unresponsive power and thus share the fate of the once mighty Roman Empire?"

Thinking of the hateful Frederick and his companions, John found himself nodding. The redcoats lodging on his family's property seemed to have no care for anyone but themselves. What cause did they give anyone to respect their position?

"Adams is right," Charles Osgood said eagerly. "I told my cousin, Samuel, that he would find much in common with the local Sons of Liberty."

"The room is full of good Patriots," Revere said with a smile. "Including our newly arrived guests." He turned toward John and George. "Tell us, friends. What is the latest word on your most interesting and important quest?"

John hesitated, glancing at George. Despite the impeccable reputations of Adams and Hancock, and Revere's obvious trust in the Osgood cousins as well, it felt strange to speak of their treasure hunt in such open company. Had it not been Revere himself who urged them to secrecy in the first place?

Still, all five men were staring at him now, clearly waiting for him to say something. So he cleared his throat and began to answer Revere's question, describing their attempts so far to figure out the most recent decoded clue, and ending by quoting it in full for the benefit of those who had not seen it.

"Wait—did you say the house of Prosperity?" Charles spoke up, stepping forward so quickly that he nearly bumped into a display of silver tankards. "I know Prosperity!"

"What?" For a moment John did not understand what he meant.

"Prosperity—*Miss* Prosperity Latham," Charles said. "She lives in one of the big houses along the Common. I know her well, for she is the only Patriot in a family of staunch Loyalists."

"Oh, of course! I should have remembered her myself," Hancock spoke up. "Young Miss Prosperity has done some spying on behalf of the Sons of Liberty. She is a fine girl, of impeccable courage and dedication."

Now the pieces were falling into place in John's head. "'The house of Prosperity by commons,'" he said. "Surely this means the treasure or the next clue is hidden within the Latham home, which as you point out Charles, happens to be located by Boston Common!"

Hancock had been leaning against a wooden table that held a selection of silver spoons. Now he let out a bark of appreciative laughter.

"Ingenious!" he exclaimed, pounding one hand on the tabletop so hard that the spoons jumped, and Revere had to step forward to catch one as it bounced right off the table. "What better spot to hide a Patriot treasure than the last place our enemies would look—within the very heart of one of their homes?"

"Ah, those Linonian lads are clever indeed," Revere agreed with a chuckle as he dropped the runaway spoon back in its place. "Whoever invented this clue must be acquainted with Miss Prosperity and knew she would help any Patriot find a way to retrieve what he is seeking."

"So what are we waiting for?" George rubbed his hands together. "Let's get over there and see what we can find!"

"Hold on a moment," John said. "All we have so far is that it's somewhere in that house. Let us see if we can not winnow it down before we go rushing in."

Hancock nodded. "What was the next bit of the clue?" he asked. "Something about the center of the realm?"

"*Within center realm therein*," John quoted.

"That sounds as if what you seek lies in the centermost chamber of the house," Revere put in. "As for the rest, the bit about the subject being the crown, that could indicate a portrait of the king or a piece of furniture displaying some sort of royal insignia."

"That does seem logical. I suppose we can look for that sort of thing once we get inside and find the correct chamber." John took a deep breath, realizing what he was saying. He and George were going to have to infiltrate the very enemy's lair—the home of wealthy Loyalists. John felt a heady mixture of excitement and pressure course through his body.

"Best of luck, boys." Adams extended his hand. "I shall be interested in hearing how your adventure turns out. Thank you for doing your part in the cause of resistance to tyranny."

John straightened his back, feeling a bit braver as he

shook Adams's hand. "Thank you, sir," he said. "We will do our best to make you proud." *I hope*, he added silently.

"There she is!" George hissed in John's ear, shaking him by the shoulder.

He and George had easily found the Latham house and were now observing it from behind the shelter of a carriage parked nearby.

"Are we certain that's her?" John stared at the girl who had just emerged to dump a pot of water in the street. She was a year or two older than he was, with rosy lips and cheeks against pale skin. Her eyes and hair were as dark as coal, and she was dressed in an expensive-looking square-necked gown of pale blue cotton.

"That Osgood chap said Prosperity has black hair and fair skin, while all her sisters have hair that is lighter in hue," George whispered back, sounding impatient. "Now, does that look like black hair to you or not?"

John made a face at him. "All right," he said. "Let's try to attract her attention before she goes back inside."

The girl had already turned back toward the door. Fearing they might miss their chance, John burst out from his hiding spot, nearly tripping over his own feet as he leaped toward her.

"Begging your pardon," he gasped out as the girl blinked at him in surprise. "Are you Miss Prosperity Latham?"

"I am," the girl replied in a rich, measured voice. "Who, may I ask, would like to know?"

John quickly introduced himself and George. "We are Patriots, here on a mission to undercover a treasure that will aid in the struggle against the Royalists," he said in a low, urgent voice. "We believe a clue to it may lie within your house. Can you help us?"

Prosperity grimaced, glancing back toward the house. "Oh, dear," she said, wrapping her arms around herself against the cold. "I have been expecting someone," she gave John a measured look, "although you are not quite what I had in mind. You could not have chosen a worse day to come. My house is currently filled up even more than usual with Tories—my father is entertaining a whole group of Loyalists and royal officers and such for the Christmas holiday. Some have come from as far as North Carolina and will be here through the week."

John's heart sank.

"I see," he said. "Well, I suppose that does present a problem."

"We cannot just give up," George argued. "Who knows when we shall have the chance to ride to Boston again? Between the weather, our duties at home, and the blasted regulars making trouble for us all, it could be spring before we could come back! And you heard the way Mr. Adams and the others were talking—spring could be too late!"

John winced, hushing his friend, whose voice had grown loud with passion. "What choice have we?" he hissed. "It is risky enough to enter a Loyalist's home. But during a party of Loyalists? It is completely foolhardy!"

"Mr. Adams?" Prosperity put in curiously. "Do you mean Mr. Samuel Adams? Has he sent you?"

"Not exactly," John said, at the same moment George replied, "Yes!"

Prosperity caught her lower lip between her teeth. Glancing again at the house behind her, she let out a sigh. "I have an idea. . . ."

"Are you certain this plan will work?" John asked, feeling foolish and conspicuous dressed in the house servant's livery

Prosperity had produced. He yanked down the sleeves of the too-small shirt, shivering. It had been a chilly matter getting changed in the open courtyard behind the house, and he was already missing his heavy winter coat. He felt a bit better when he glanced over at George, whose disguise was even more ill-fitting than his own. He laughed, earning him a disgruntled look from his friend.

"Nothing in this life is certain," Prosperity said calmly. "Now I must return before I am missed." She turned away, then paused and looked back. "Oh, be certain to avoid catching the eye of the skinny fellow with a scar on one cheek. He is the head of the servants here and was solely charged with hiring on the extras for this party. He will know you do not belong."

"Wonderful," George muttered as Prosperity hurried off and disappeared through a door. "I still do not see why that girl could not retrieve the clue and bring it to us outside."

"We could not let her risk being caught doing so. She is of too much value to the Sons of Liberty as a spy." John shrugged. "In any case, at least now we know what we are seeking. All we must do is make our way to the small chamber at the center of the house and find that sampler, and then we can depart."

While Prosperity was helping to disguise them, she'd told them where to find the next clue. "It is hidden behind a sampler I made a year or two back," she said. "The subject of the sampler is the glory of King George and our benefi-cent English sovereign state." She pulled a horrible face to indicate her disapproval. "My mother forced me to stitch it, and I despised every moment of the work." Her expression softened into a mischievous smile. "That is why I was quick to offer it as a hiding place when Robert mentioned he needed a spot where no one would ever be likely to look. The sampler hangs in a gloomy and little-used room."

"Robert?" John had asked Prosperity curiously.

She had explained that Robert was a young man of her acquaintance who had grown up nearby and had often returned to visit his family during his years at Yale. Currently he was living in another part of Boston, estranged from his Loyalist family due to his fervent support for the Sons of Liberty.

"I suppose Mr. Revere was correct in guessing that many hands went into this trail we are following," John murmured now, speaking more to himself than to George as the two of them walked across the courtyard toward the kitchen door.

"Hush," George warned. "Try to act like a house servant."

Prosperity had explained that all they had to do was cross the kitchen and go through the doorway on the left-hand side. They would then find themselves in the small chamber behind the room where the sampler hung.

In the kitchen, they found a scene of chaos. A pair of red-faced, sweating servant women were stirring large pots over the fire while others arranged food on platters; and several young men hurried in and out of a door in the right-hand wall near the hearth with more platters and big pitchers of drink. The enticing scents of cooking meat and burnt sugar mingled with the everyday odors of sweat and smoke.

John glanced around for any sign of a man with a scar. But aside from the young servers, the rest of the kitchen's inhabitants were all female. "Let's go!" he whispered to George, nodding to what he hoped was the correct door.

They started across the room, barely dodging a servant staggering beneath the weight of a roasted goose on a platter. A couple others glanced toward them curiously, but all seemed too busy to wonder much about the newcomers' identities.

They were halfway to the door when a small, thin man rushed in. A jagged white scar gleamed out clearly from his sallow-complected face. John gulped. Grabbing George, he yanked him through the door in the left wall before the man could spot them.

They found themselves in a quiet, narrow chamber that appeared to be used as a sort of office or library, with an impressive mahogany desk and several shelves full of books. There was no one else present.

"That was close." John whispered. "Perhaps if we wait a moment, he will go out again, and we can continue on our way."

George nodded and glanced around curiously. "Yes," he said. "Or, we could get inside that central chamber now."

Before John could protest, George was already hurrying toward another doorway at the far end of the room.

"If I understood Prosperity correctly," he said, "the chamber we want should be right about—here!"

He swung open the door. John peered over his shoulder.

"There it is!" he exclaimed. Hanging on the opposite wall was a large sampler. In addition to the usual alphabet and other stitchwork motifs, it featured a golden-colored crown right in the middle, which showed up clearly against the background fabric even in the relatively dim light of the windowless room.

The two friends hurried toward it. John felt excited. "Prosperity said the clue is—" John began. But he did not have a chance to finish.

"What are you two doing in here?" a voice boomed out suddenly.

Fifteen

John stopped short in the middle of the room. A portly gentleman had just entered through another door at the far end. He was peering at them in confusion.

"B-begging your pardon, sir," John stammered. His mind raced, but his body felt frozen in place. What now? Would the man deduce their deception? Beside him, George seemed frozen as well.

The man didn't wait for their response. "We have been waiting a king's age for the marzipan," he said sternly. With one fat finger, he pointed at the door in the side wall, which John assumed was the one that led directly into the kitchen. "Now get in there and fetch it immediately, or you'll be out on the street with no pay!"

John gulped. On the one hand, it was a relief that the man clearly had no trouble believing they were servants, despite their ill-fitting uniforms. On the other, if that fellow with the scar was still in the kitchen when they entered, the ruse would surely be revealed.

At that moment Prosperity appeared in the doorway behind the man. An expression of alarm flashed across her face when she saw John and George, but it was gone as quickly as it had come, replaced by a fond smile.

"Ah, there you are, Father," she said, taking the man by the arm and peering up at him engagingly. "Mrs. Wendall is most eager to hear the tale of your latest journey to London."

Mr. Latham's expression softened immediately into one of doting affection. "Of course, my pet. I shall be right there. I only wish to ensure that these houseboys are doing the job for which I am paying them."

"I shall see to it for you, Father," Prosperity assured him, carefully steering him back out the door. "Rest easy about that."

A moment later Mr. Latham was gone. Prosperity ducked back into the room just long enough to whisper the word "Hurry!" before disappearing as well.

When she was gone, John grabbed the sampler and flipped it over. There was a small, folded piece of paper stuck into the back of its wooden frame, and John quickly removed it and stuffed it into his clothes.

"Come," he told George, who looked rather paler than usual after the close call. "Let's get out of here."

A short while later they were back out in the cold early evening air, dressed in their own clothes. They hurried side by side across the Common without daring to look back; John didn't know what his friend was thinking, but for his part he took every step expecting to hear the voice of Prosperity's father barking after them again.

They waited until they reached the street on the far side of the Common before they dared to speak. And even then, they did not stop but continued on through the maze of streets until they were well out of sight of the Latham house. Finally, they paused on a deserted corner to look at the clue. It held only a single line:

Here Liberty grows in Blaxton's home.

"Blaxton," George said. "Do you suppose that's another friend of these Sons of Liberty? Or one of those Linonian chaps?"

John did not know and as both he and George had promised their families to try to return before Christmas

Day, they had no choice but to ride for Concord—the latest clue unsolved.

Christmas passed as it generally did in the New England colonies: with little fanfare. John's family, being originally from much farther south, did enjoy a special meal to mark the occasion, though it was perhaps less festive than in earlier years due both to the holiday's connection with England and the presence of the redcoats in the stable just outside their doors.

By the first week of the New Year the holidays were forgotten and life returned to its normal pace, John found his post-rider duties increasing, which meant little time for treasure hunting. Reality was far too pressing.

One day, in mid-January, he returned from a wearying journey to Scituate to find the odious Frederick standing in the courtyard in front of the stable staring at the house and scratching his belly.

"Ah, there you are, boy," the soldier said in an insolent tone as John swung down from Liberty's back. "I have been waiting an age for the comely Alice to return. Go and see what is keeping her."

John gritted his teeth. It was growing harder and harder to tolerate the unwelcome strangers in their stable. "I need to tend to my horse," he said in as neutral a tone as he could manage. "You shall just have to wait a bit longer."

"How dare you!" Frederick's ruddy face instantly went dark, and he drew himself up to his full, rather impressive height. "That was an order from one of the king's men! Dare ye to defy it, boy? Now, I told you once to go and fetch Alice—must I repeat myself?"

"Here I am!" Alice hurried in at that moment bearing a tray of boiled meat. "No need for shouting, sir."

Frederick's glowering face relaxed immediately into a smile. "Ah, Miss Alice," he said. "You do look lovely when you hurry, as you do at all other times as well. But please— I have insisted several times now that you call me by my given name."

"Of course—Frederick." Alice blushed slightly and glanced down at her feet. "I keep forgetting. It comes so naturally for me to address you by a more respectful title befitting your position."

"That is all right," the soldier replied magnanimously, reaching for the tray. "Now, I do hope you shall do me the pleasure of remaining with me while I eat. . . ."

John felt his blood start to boil. How dare Frederick take that impertinent tone with his sister? And worse yet, Alice seemed not to mind at all! She giggled and curtsied, then followed Frederick over to the crude plank table and benches that he and his comrades had set up outside one of their sleeping stalls.

This is outrageous, he thought, tugging at Liberty's reins to lead her away where he would not have to witness any more. *It is bad enough to be forced to wait upon these louts in our very home. But watching Alice seem to enjoy such torture is doubly vexing! It is time I had a word with her about this. . . .*

He got his chance to speak with her privately late the next afternoon, when he came upon her breaking ice in the water dish in the henhouse. Glancing around to make certain that they were alone, he hurried over.

"What can you be thinking?" he blurted out in way of greeting. "How can you tolerate the crude advances of *Frederick*? Are you—you can't actually have feelings for that disgusting Tory, can you?"

Alice straightened up and looked at him. "Please, John," she said with a snort. "Do you really think me so lacking in discrimination? I abhor him as much as anyone."

"Well, one wouldn't know it by the way you have been acting!" John said, all the indignation of the past few weeks bubbling over in his voice and expression. "Every time I see you lately, you are laughing at his idiotic jokes or blushin as you accept his compliments! It is revolting!"

"Indeed, you are correct, brother. I *have* been feigning a tolerance for the man," Alice said calmly. "I have discovered that by acting thusly, he is willing to reveal to me all sorts of things that he probably should not." She glanced at John with a sly smile. "It is not only you brave post riders and Minutemen who are willing to do your part for the rebellion."

John stared at her for a moment, unsure. Then his outrage melted away as he realized what she was telling him. He smiled and shook his head.

"I am sorry to have doubted you, Alice," he said. "I should have guessed it had to be something like that." He shuddered. "In fact, I am beginning to think you a stronger Patriot than I. For I would sooner allow myself to be shot by all the king's men than spend one unnecessary moment being nice to one such as Frederick!"

"Hush." Alice's teasing smile vanished at the sound of footsteps. Glancing over her shoulder she added, "Here he comes."

John turned to see Frederick swaggering toward them across the snow-covered kitchen garden. "Ah, there you are, my sweet Alice," he said. "That one-handed sister of yours said I might find you out here. I am in need of food. I am exhausted and hungry after spending much of the day beating some sense into several local sympathizers of the Sons of *Iniquity*."

With a wince, John wondered which of his Patriot neighbors had fallen victim to the redcoats' bullying this time. Frederick and his friends were certainly making themselves unpopular around Concord.

"John, are you out here?" Thomas Gates hurried out of the house at that moment. "I just heard from Mr. Jackson that he and Sims and some others encountered the regulars, and—oh." He stopped short when he noticed Frederick. "Er, never mind. It can wait."

"Good." Frederick stared at him with his usual vapid expression. "Because while the sight of your daughter's adoring face has refreshed me a bit, I am still in need of sustenance. She was just about to fetch me some food and drink." He leaned closer to Alice and gave her a squeeze on the backside. "Get after that now, will you, love?"

"Right away, Frederick," Alice said brightly. "I shall bring it to your lodgings presently." She hurried past her father into the house.

Thomas glanced after her, then back at Frederick. For a moment, John saw an expression of fury cross his father's face. But it was gone almost instantly, replaced by a sort of weary sadness.

As Frederick marched off toward the stable and Thomas turned back toward the house, John was tempted to follow his father and assure him that Alice had no positive feelings toward the oafish regular. But he forced himself to keep quiet, merely watching Thomas disappear back inside. It was not, after all, his secret to reveal.

As the long, cold Massachusetts days wore on, John and George met as often as they could to discuss the clue they had discovered at Prosperity's house. However, aside from the occasional chance meeting at the tavern, they saw little of Duncan during this time. John knew that one reason for this remained the same as ever—even as the village and surrounding areas became more deeply divided between Loyalist and Patriot, Duncan's family still clung stubbornly to the idea of neutrality.

But John had come to suspect there might be another reason for his friend's absence as well. On his last visit to John's home, Duncan had been witness to one of Frederick's encounters with Alice. Ever since, the very mention of her name had caused a shadow to fall over his face. At first John had not understood what this might mean. But eventually an explanation dawned on him. Could Duncan—shy, quiet, bookish Duncan—be entertaining feelings toward Alice? It was an interesting thought, if one that seemed unlikely to go anywhere at the moment. John only hoped his young friend was not too heartsick—after all, Alice's behavior was nothing but an elaborate ruse.

Then one day in mid-February John and George were chipping frozen manure out of one of the stalls in the Gates family stable when Duncan suddenly burst in. "I've got it!" he cried with great excitement. Suddenly catching himself, he glanced around cautiously. "The lobsterbacks aren't here, are they?"

"No," George replied. "They are out causing trouble in the village, as usual."

"Good." Duncan's smile returned, even brighter. "Because I figured out part of the clue!"

"You did?" John straightened up and mopped his forehead, which was sweaty with exertion despite the bitter temperature. "What is it?"

"I am convinced that it refers to William Blaxton, who first settled the land that became Boston back in the 1620s," Duncan said. "I had forgotten his name, but recently came across it in a book."

John nodded. "Sounds reasonable. But what does it mean? Does Blaxton's original home still stand in Boston?"

"I doubt that," Duncan said. "Indeed, I think the rest of the clue is pointing us elsewhere. The clue said, 'Here Liberty grows.' That seems to indicate a specific location within Boston—Blaxton's home. Perhaps the Old South Meeting House . . ."

George nodded. "Or it could be a certain lesser known meeting place that would be familiar only to Patriots."

"Grows," John said thoughtfully, hardly hearing what his friends were saying. "Where Liberty *grows*. It is an odd choice of words. Unless—could it refer to the Liberty Tree?"

"Of course!" Duncan smacked himself in the head. "Why didn't I think of that?"

Nearly every town in Massachusetts had its own Liberty Tree or Liberty Pole by then; Concord had itself recently erected such a pole. But all were copies of the famous old elm that stood near Boston Common. Since the days of the Stamp Act, the great tree had been a rallying spot for Patriots and a living symbol of their cause. Naturally, the creators of this trail would use the Liberty Tree as one of their clues!

John was only sorry that he hadn't seen it sooner. He realized that the quest—and even his interest in political matters in general—had become somewhat dormant within him while he was otherwise occupied with the everyday business of dealing with Frederick and his ilk and surviving another harsh New England winter. But now the passion flared up within him once more.

"We must ride for Boston again as soon as possible!" he exclaimed, determined to make up for lost time.

Unfortunately, "as soon as possible" turned out not to be very soon at all. It was more than a fortnight before the three friends were able to arrange another journey to the city. But finally, one crisp morning in early March, they all met at the stable. It was just before dawn, and they kept their voices down as they converged in the courtyard.

"Did you have any trouble slipping away?" George asked Duncan.

Duncan shook his head. "I told my family I am riding to Medford to return a book I borrowed from a friend there. They shall never need to know my true errand."

"Good." John shot a nervous glance toward the interior of the stable, from which emitted both the sort whickers of the horses and the snores of the redcoats. "Come, let's be off before the lobsterbacks awaken and start ordering us about."

He fetched Salem first, and then left George helping Duncan to mount while returning for Red, George's horse for the trip. Finally, he returned into the stable once more, heading for the stall where he'd left Liberty finishing her breakfast about an hour earlier. But when he reached the stall, it was empty.

"What?" he cried aloud, staring about as if an entire horse could somehow hide in a corner or crawl beneath the boards and into the next stall. "Where did she go?"

"S'gone," said a sleepy voice behind him.

Turning, John saw one of Frederick's buddies standing there, dressed only in his shift and yawning widely. "What?"

"Frederick had some business over in Lexington." The soldier, a rather fat young man named Edward, paused to yawn again, sending a whiff of stale breath John's way. "He heard your old man tell someone that mare was the fastest horse on the place, so he took her."

Sixteen

John was furious. "What do you mean, he took her?" he shouted. "How dare he! You all act as if this place is your own property, and we nothing but your servants, but I am here to tell you—"

"What's going on in here?" Suddenly George was there beside him, pulling him away from the soldier. It wasn't until then that John realized he'd grabbed Edward by the collar of his shift. "Come, John. Let's settle down—no harm done, eh?"

Edward frowned and adjusted his shift. "This is an outrage," he grumbled. "I am a member of the king's army and deserve some respect."

"Of course," George said through gritted teeth. "It was all a misunderstanding. My friend is, er, very attached to that particular mare, that's all."

"But—" John protested.

George didn't give him a chance to continue, instead

yanking him around the corner into the tack room. "Are you mad?" he hissed. "If you get those fellows all riled up, we'll never make it to Boston today and you'll risk punishment!"

John's shoulders slumped as he realized his friend was right. As much as he despised the thought of the hateful Frederick riding his favorite mare, there wasn't much he could do about it.

"Well, I hope she bucks him off and breaks his fool neck," he muttered.

"That's the spirit." George grinned and slapped him on the back. "Now come—I'll help you saddle up another horse."

"It is too bad we didn't figure out the clue immediately upon seeing it," George commented as the three friends dismounted on Essex Street in Boston sometime later. "We walked within a few blocks of the Liberty Tree, leaving the Latham house."

"Indeed." John stared at the large oak growing nearby, its branches bare of leaves and stretching toward the iron gray winter sky. "Then again, we would have had to approach it in full view of that household full of Loyalists."

Duncan glanced around. "Luckily, there don't seem to be many lobsterbacks around today," he said. "Perhaps they were scared off by the cold."

It was indeed a cold day, the brisk wind off the harbor chasing the few pedestrians along at top speed and keeping most other people indoors. Nobody paid the boys any notice as they walked up to the tree, leading their horses.

"Now what?" George stared up into the branches. "Do we look for something carved in the trunk?"

"Perhaps." John examined the trunk carefully. Several wind-whipped leaflets hung there, along with an abandoned lantern, and a few people had indeed carved things into the bark, though none appeared to be clues.

"Should we write down everything that's here?" George asked uncertainly, staring at a leaflet for some long-finished meeting.

Duncan was staring upward. "No, wait," he said. "Do you see that? A flash of silver—up there!"

John looked up into the branches, the more slender of which were waving gently with each new gust of wind. "Where?" he asked, squinting.

Duncan pointed. "Up there," he said. "Right where

that crooked branch meets the trunk—do you see?"

George gasped. "I see it! Do you think it could be the clue?"

John had spotted it by now, too. "One way to find out," he said. Shedding his overcoat, he grabbed the trunk and started shimmying up, keeping his eyes on that flash of silver.

A few minutes later he was climbing down again, a small silver box clutched tightly in one hand. "Let's see it!" Duncan cried eagerly.

John brushed off his hands and clothes. Then he opened the box. "What a surprise," he joked when he saw what was inside. "Another piece of paper!"

He unfolded it. Again, they found a clue consisting of only one sentence:

Find ye my sister like the Colonel's good Nelson in the place of our first covenant.

"What do you suppose is the meaning of *this* one?" George asked, not hiding his annoyance. Each time they took one step forward, a new clue set them back two.

Noticing that Duncan's thin shoulders were shivering badly despite his heavy clothes, John walked over and stuck both box and clue into his saddlebags. "I don't know," he said, equally frustrated. "Let's go find somewhere to discuss it over a warm drink."

By the time they'd thawed themselves at the nearest tavern, the boys were no closer to any answers. They argued a bit over what to do next—George was in favor of staying in Boston a bit longer to save themselves yet another trip in case the clue was pointing them somewhere else within the city. But John could tell that Duncan was anxious about being found out by his family if he was away too long, and so they eventually decided to head back home.

They discussed the clue all the way back to Concord and at every opportunity thereafter. But again, days turned into weeks without them hitting upon any answers. For John, the latest cryptic line became an obsession that filled his mind at nearly every waking moment. What Colonel? Who was Nelson? Whose sister? Which covenant? The questions circled in his head endlessly.

Nearly the only thing that distracted him was the

continuing irksome presence of Frederick and the other regulars. Every time he went out to the stable to feed the horses or clean the stalls, the men were there smirking at him or ordering him to fetch more food and beer. Worse yet, every time he went to the tavern lately he seemed to hear whispers about Alice. His sister Mary had heard them, too.

"What is to be done about that girl?" she commented to John one day, twisting a finger in her auburn curls as was her habit in moments of anxiety. "The whole town is starting to talk. Why, Oliver and I were even accused of being Tories ourselves last evening! I thought Oliver might strike the man who said it!"

John knew how Oliver had felt. The Gates family didn't have the best reputation as it was, thanks to Thomas's lifetime of fruitless treasure hunting. Even though he knew Alice was doing, John wished she would stop humoring Frederick's advances, especially in public. It would be unbearable if the family's neighbors truly started thinking of them—even only *one* of them—as possible Loyalist sympathizers!

Despite the concerns at home, life—and work—went

on. One day in late March, John was hired to carry a sack full of letters to several towns in the vicinity of Springfield. After dropping off the last batch at the inn at Southwick, he turned his weary horse toward Justin Morgan's stables.

He arrived to find Mr. Morgan hard at work chipping ice out of his water troughs. "Young Gates!" Morgan exclaimed, as usual seeming delighted to see him. "It is always a pleasure to have a visit from you."

"And you as well, sir. Can you help my poor horse? I'm afraid I have ridden him a long way this day."

"Of course, of course." Morgan helped John untack his tired mount, stow him in a spare stall, and give him hay and water.

Once that was settled, Morgan invited John inside to warm up and rest. Soon they were sitting before the fire in Morgan's small but tidy keeping room. His wife was not at home at the moment, and so the two of them were free to discuss horses along with any other matters they pleased.

The talk eventually turned to politics. Until that day, John had discussed such matters with Morgan only in the most general terms. He was not even entirely certain of the man's leanings, though he found it distressing to consider even the possibility that his mild-mannered, intelligent, amiable friend might be a Loyalist.

But as soon as Morgan made his Patriot leanings clear, John's mind once again filled up with that infernal clue. He and his friends weren't having much luck in solving it, and there was no telling when they might again make it to Boston to discuss it with Mr. Revere and the other Sons of Liberty. Perhaps it was time to look for help elsewhere. And why not begin with Mr. Morgan? He had always struck John as the clever sort.

"Here's something of interest," he said, reaching for the clue, which he kept always upon his person. "It is a—a sort of puzzle."

"A-ha!" Morgan leaned forward with a smile. "Let me guess. It is that father of yours, yes? He is forever trying to trick me with his codes and riddles!"

John chuckled weakly, not bothering to correct the man's impression. It was probably best if Morgan stayed slightly ignorant of the clue's true origin.

"I'd be interested to see what you can make of it."

Morgan took the piece of paper and peered at it. He read through it once, his lips moving along with his eyes, then glanced up at John with a smile.

"Well, I suppose you've figured out this part already, have you?" he commented, tapping one long, slender, work-worn finger on the page.

"Which part?" John asked. "We have not figured out anything."

Morgan raised one eyebrow in surprise. "Ah, but I was certain a horseman such as yourself would see it," he said. "Surely this note must refer to Colonel Washington's best horse, the handsome chestnut he calls Nelson."

"He does?" John blinked, the familiar twinge of excitement flaring up. Showing the clue to Morgan *had* been the right decision. How many men would know the appellation of the well-known political leader's favorite mount? He himself had not, and he considered himself horseman and Patriot both!

They chatted a bit more about the rest of the clue, but Morgan soon began to seem distracted. Guessing that his host was thinking of the chores still awaiting him in the barn, John rose and prepared to depart. A short while later he set out on the road again on a fresh horse—and with renewed energy for his quest as well.

✳ ✳ ✳

The piece of information about Nelson the horse turned out to be just the push that John and his friends needed. Over the course of the next week or two, they managed to puzzle out the rest of the clue. It was the sometimes fanciful-minded Duncan who first theorized that the clue could be written as if by the Liberty Tree itself, meaning the "sister" it referenced could indicate another tree. George had often teased John by saying that one or another of his stable's chestnut horses was as nutty as a chestnut tree, and so it was he who deduced that the tree they were seeking must be a chestnut, as that was the color of Washington's horse according to Mr. Morgan.

"So it is another Liberty Tree we are seeking," John said as he and his friends sat huddled over the clue in the harness shop. All the redcoats were off at a muster, so they were able to talk freely without looking over their shoulders at every moment.

"A Liberty Tree that is also a chestnut," Duncan agreed, rubbing his chin thoughtfully. "The question remains where. What is meant by 'in the place of our first covenant?' Is it Boston again, where the Sons of Liberty began? Could there be another Liberty Tree elsewhere in the city?"

The same questions had been on John's mind for days. "First covenant," he said. "What would those words mean to a well-educated Patriot?"

He squeezed his eyes shut, trying to recall the information in some of the books of history that he and Alice had read to each other in front of the fire in years past. Why hadn't he paid more attention?

"Wait!" he said, his eyes flying open as the memory he was seeking finally floated to the fore. "Wasn't there a sort of governing contract, a code of laws that was written by the first settlers in New England in the last century?"

George just shrugged, but Duncan nodded. "I have heard it called the Mayflower Compact, named for the ship on which those settlers came," he said. "But how—oh, I see!"

"The Mayflower settlers," John said. "They landed in Plymouth, is that right?" He smiled. "That's the answer, then. The tree we seek must be in Plymouth! We must ride there immediately!"

But before his friends could respond, there was a sudden burst of shouts from the courtyard just outside. "What's going on?" George wondered, leading the way as they all headed out in that direction.

They found Thomas facing off against a small band of their neighbors, led by a grim-faced Mr. Sims. "What is the meaning of this?" Thomas demanded, crossing his arms over his chest.

"We need to talk to you, Gates," Sims retorted, to many nods and some grumbling from the rest. "It's about your daughter Alice."

Seventeen

"I have nothing to say to the likes of you, Sims," Thomas growled. "My family is my own business; it's none of yours."

"The behavior of traitors is the business of us all!" called out a man near the back of the group, a stout farmer named Williams. "In these times we cannot afford to have such turncoats in our midst. At least the lobsterbacks are recognized by their red coats—not so for Tories who pose as one of us!"

"We have all seen them together, Gates," added the local barber. "Your daughter and that insufferable lobsterback. It is the talk of the village."

John wanted to say something to defend his family. But before he could do so, Thomas let out a loud oath. His face had gone red and his eyes were all but shooting fire.

"Is this how you practice liberty?" he shouted. "By trying to intimidate your neighbors—those who have lived among you all your lives? If so, I have no use for you, no matter who or what you say you support! Now get off my property before I throw you off myself!"

For a long, tense moment the men remained, glaring at Thomas, who glared back. John glanced at his friends. Duncan looked pale and nervous, and George had taken half a step forward and was staring at Thomas with confusion, as if not certain whether to defend him or not.

But finally, it was Sims who backed down. "Come along, men," he grumbled. "It is clear we are wasting our time here."

It wasn't until they'd all disappeared over the rise in the road that John felt himself relax. He let out the breath he hadn't realized he'd been holding and glanced over at his father. Thomas didn't meet his eye. Muttering something about checking on the colt, he stalked off into the stable.

Luckily the incident seemed to blow over for the most part. The next time John encountered Mr. Williams at the tavern, the man greeted him as if it had never happened. But if nothing else, the confrontation had showed John just how tense things were. It made him feel as if all of Concord were a tinderbox waiting only for a spark to cause it to explode into flames. And not just Concord, but Massachusetts beyond that, and perhaps all the colonies. That feeling made it seem all the more urgent to get to Plymouth and solve the puzzle as soon as possible. If the "treasure" was to aid the Patriots, it seemed best they find it.

George was required to remain in Concord for the next several days due to training sessions, but he insisted the others go without him. So John and Duncan set out the very next morning, once again inventing stories to explain their absence.

It was a very long ride to Plymouth. But when they arrived the next day, they had no trouble finding the tree in question. Located in a meadow on the edge of the town, the Plymouth Liberty Tree was a proud chestnut festooned with leaflets, cartoons, and other messages, the flag of the Sons of Liberty dangling from one of its large branches.

"I hope we do not have to copy down all that is written here," Duncan said, peering warily at the dozens of pages fluttering wildly in the breeze coming off the bay.

Meanwhile John was peering upward something catching the sunlight in the upper branches. "I think not," he said. "At least, not if that is what I think it is. . . ."

It was; a small pewter snuff box was hidden in much the

same spot as the other had been in the Boston tree. When John returned with it to the ground, he opened it and found another note:

> If ye be one of Barré's Boys, know ye the name of Maryland's "First Citizen." His father's appellation from here shall help ye reach the mark as the sun rises to shine upon the glory of this Patriot's land.

John stared down at it with a sigh. "Barré's Boys, First Citizen, Maryland . . . Will these infernal clues never end?" he muttered.

But Duncan shrugged. "At least this one seems more clearly to be directing us to a mark which might mean an end," he said. "We need only figure out where. And I already know the answer to part of it—I believe Isaac Barré is a member of Parliament who opposes taxation of the colonies; it was from one of his speeches that the Sons of Liberty took their name." He grinned at John. "See? We must be getting better at this!"

John laughed. "Come," he said, knowing that it was a long ride back to Concord, and they didn't dare stay away too long. "Let's find ourselves some fresh horses and ride for home. Perhaps George can help us figure out the rest."

"Where is it?" George burst into the stable the morning after their return from Plymouth. "Duncan said you found—" He stopped himself, then glanced around cautiously. "Er, is anyone else about?"

"No, Frederick and the rest of his group are not here," John replied, dropping the bridle he was oiling and rubbing his hands on a rag. "And yes—we did find another clue. But where is Duncan? Did he not come with you?"

George grimaced. "I am afraid not," he said. "His father spoke to someone who witnessed you two riding off the other day to the southeast, rather than Duncan riding alone to the west as he had claimed he was doing. He is now forbidden to mix with rebellious influences such as ourselves. 'Until things settle down around here,' as I think his father put it."

"That could be a long while indeed." John felt a flash of guilt for getting his friend in trouble. But knowing Duncan as he did, he knew he probably didn't regret it at all and would do it again if asked.

He pulled out the clue and showed it to George, explaining what Duncan had deduced about the reference to Barré's Boys. "Why can't these Yale fellows write in plain English?" George grumbled as he read over the rest.

John chuckled. "Ah, but then even the doltish regulars might stumble upon the—"

"Is anyone about?" a gruff voice shouted from just outside, interrupting him. "We are in need of sustenance."

"Frederick," John said, pronouncing the name as if it were an oath. He tucked away the clue and sighed. How could Alice stand to be around the brutish redcoat so much even for good cause? "I'd better go see what he wants."

As the first week of April came and went, John and his friends continued to puzzle over the clue. Duncan was still banned from seeing the others, but he managed to sneak out long enough to meet them at the tavern and tell them he'd figured out another part of the message.

"I thought the 'First Citizen' bit seemed familiar," he told them, his slender fingers drumming on the table as his eyes darted here and there in search of anyone who might give him away to his father. "Do you recall the controversy a couple of years back in which an anonymous person debated against the secretary of Maryland Colony in their local newspapers on matters of taxation?"

"No," George said, and John shrugged.

Duncan rolled his eyes before going on. "Well, in any case, it was widely reported even this far north, if one *happened* to be paying attention," he jibed. "The anonymous writer was later revealed to be Mr. Charles Carroll, the Catholic intellectual and champion of independence. But at the time he signed himself only with the pseudonym 'First Citizen.'"

"I see!" John nodded with interest. "But do you know the name of his father? The clue mentions 'his father's appellation.' What do you suppose that means?"

"I do not know." Duncan pushed himself to his feet with his cane. "But I shall leave you two to figure it out. I have been away from home too long already."

"Where is Alice?" John asked his father and Elizabeth, who were both in the kitchen when he returned home. He was eager to tell her of Duncan's idea and see what she thought. She had been so busy looking after Frederick's every whim that it had been difficult to find a moment alone with her, but he had finally managed to show her the clue the previous day while the regulars were out with the rest of their comrades.

"She is out in the stable tending to our . . . visitors." Elizabeth's tone was calm, though her eyes were troubled. "I was expecting her in with the water some time ago."

John bit his lip, momentarily forgetting the clue in a new wave of worry over his sister's reckless behavior. "Father," he said, "can you not speak to her about being more circumspect? You already know people are beginning to talk."

"So let people talk," Thomas said brusquely. "It will not be the first time fools have gossiped about the Gates family. And there are more pressing matters to worry over at the moment."

He stalked out of the room without further comment. John stared after him, barely hearing Elizabeth scolding him gently for upsetting him. Something about his father's expression had reminded him of the day Thomas had sent that Lexington Minuteman on his way without asking for payment. And the more pressing matters he mentioned? Could he be referring to the greater conflict brewing beyond their own small town?

John's eyes grew wide. And in that moment, all his doubts about his father's political stance melted away like the heavy snows of the past months. He realized that in his own gruff, quiet way, Thomas was as much a Patriot as he was himself. Why hadn't he seen it before?

A few days later, John accompanied his sisters to Sunday meeting at the church, though Thomas had disappeared early that morning and was nowhere to be found when they left the house. They soon joined Mary and Oliver, who were already seated on one of the hard wooden benches inside, and before long the minister began his duties. He droned on about heaven and hell and various related matters, and before long John found his eyelids drooping. He fought against the ever increasing waves of boredom and weariness, first by trying to sit up straighter and listen, and then, when that failed, by thinking about the still only partially solved clue.

But finally he lost the battle and slumped down in his seat, fast asleep.

He dreamed that he entered Mr. Revere's silver shop in Boston and found a series of three large doors set into its back wall. He turned to Revere in confusion, only to find

Revere had morphed into Samuel Adams, who was twelve feet tall with a great gray mane of hair and eyes that flashed fire. *You must choose your door, young Gates!* the giant Adams had thundered. *One leads to heaven, the realm of Patriots and innocent children. Another leads to hell, the dominion of Loyalists and regulars.* John had pointed to the doors. *But there are three,* he had said. *Where does the other lead?* Adams had glared at him as if thinking he should already know the answer. *No man knows where that door leads,* he said, *for it is the door of natives, neutrals, Papists, and everyone else of uncertain moral fate.* At that, John had let out a gasp. *A-ha!* he had said, just before coming suddenly awake. . . .

"That's it!" he cried aloud, sitting bolt upright.

It was only then that he realized he still sat in the church among all his family and neighbors. His cheeks grew hot as people turned to see who had interrupted the sermon. Elizabeth, who had been sitting beside him hanging on the preacher's every word, stared at him in shock. Several soft *tut-tuts* came from the surrounding benches.

"Begging your pardon," John blurted out as the minister peered down at him. "Er, I was simply overwhelmed with your words, sir. I am sorry."

A tiny girl a few rows up stood on the bench to stare at him. But John hardly noticed. Slouching in his seat, he did his best to keep the excited grin from his face, for he had just solved another part of the clue.

"Charles Carroll is a Catholic, remember?" John told George, hurrying to keep up with his friend's brisk stride. "Duncan mentioned it the other day. Could not the reference to his father indicate what the papists would surely see as his *Holy* Father—the pope?"

George stopped short. John had found him on his way to meet his brigade to help move some munitions stores, but now he seemed to forget all about that.

"That is brilliant!" he said. "You know, John, some days I think you are nearly as clever as Duncan! I never would have figured that out. So what is the name of the current Pope?"

"Ah, but it is not the current pope we want, but the one who was in power when our trail was laid," John said. "That pope died just this past September—I remember seeing it in the papers at the time." He grinned. "He was known to his followers as Clement the Fourteenth."

"Clement the Fourteenth—what a coincidence! Today is the fourteenth day of the month of April, is it not?" George grinned. Then understanding dawned on his face. "Oh! Could that number be the appellation we want? What was the rest—'this appellation shall help you find the mark,' or something like that?"

"The 'appellation from here shall help ye reach the mark,'" John quoted. "From here . . . from *here*?" He took a deep breath, realizing what that meant. "We have to go back to Plymouth," he declared. "The spot we want is there, just fourteen paces from that chestnut tree!"

Eighteen

The next morning John headed out to the stable earlier than usual to finish his chores in preparation for the ride to Plymouth. To his surprise, Frederick and the other regulars were already up. John winced when they saw him, expecting them to order him to fetch them beer and breakfast—and, in Frederick's case, to insist that he send out Alice as well.

It was another surprise, therefore, when they completely ignored him. They were getting dressed and muttering amongst themselves, their faces serious. John felt a wave of nervousness wash over him. Thinking back now, he realized that their unwelcome guests had seemed more somber than usual these past few days. Was something afoot?

He finished his chores, then returned to the house for a quick breakfast. When he returned, the redcoats were gone. But a few minutes later as he was preparing Liberty for the day's ride, George burst in, red-faced and breathless.

"There you are!" John said, casting a cautious glance

around to be sure no one was about. "Did you see Duncan? Can he come to Plymouth today?"

"No, and neither can I," George replied, gulping in air. "I am sorry, John. But the militia officers have ordered us to remain on alert. There is word from all around that the political situation is critical." He shrugged. "Duncan's father has heard the rumors, too. He is keeping a close eye on the whole family. Duncan is not allowed to leave his sight. I fear there may not be much time left; some of my fellow Minutemen are even beginning to mutter of open revolution. I think you should ride for Plymouth today as planned. If what we are seeking through these clues is as important as the Sons of Liberty seem to think . . ."

"You are right," John said, nodding.

George shook his hand. "Good luck, my friend. I shall see you when you return."

John rode steadily through the daylight hours, stopping to spend the night in Braintree. The next morning he left Liberty at a post stable there to rest until he passed by again on his way home. He continued on to Plymouth aboard a good-looking light bay horse. However, the creature was not nearly as fit as the stablekeeper had promised, which forced John to make frequent stops along the way. Even so, he arrived in the bayside village a few minutes before sunset and immediately made his way to the Liberty Tree.

The afternoon had turned raw and chilly, and nobody was about. The wind whipped the bare branches of the Liberty Tree along with those in the forest that loomed at one end of the meadow in which it grew. It also carried the woodsmoke from the fires of the houses at the other end of the meadow, making John cough. But he ignored all that, leaving his horse to crop at the remains of the dead winter grass while he stepped up to the tree.

His stomach tightened into a nervous knot. Had he and George interpreted the last clue correctly? And if they had not, what would he find . . .

Pushing his doubts aside, he took a deep breath, which made him cough again. Then he pressed his back against the trunk of the tree, looked out, and frowned.

"In which direction do I go?" he murmured.

Aside from his horse, who merely flicked an ear in his direction, there was no one to answer him. John bit his lip, thinking back over the clue once again. He glanced around, squinting against the bright pink-orange rays of the setting sun. . . .

"That's it!" he exclaimed, this time loudly enough to cause his horse to raise its head and stare at him in alarm.

John grinned. *As the sun rises to shine upon this land,* he thought. *Of course! That must indicate the direction! I am to measure the paces toward the east, the sunrise.*

Facing away from the sun now setting in the west, he found himself looking out toward the wild, shadowy forest just a short distance away. The last of the sunlight slanted in among the thick-trunked trees, creating puddles of red light in the underbrush and glinting off the large rocks scattered here and there.

"One," John counted aloud, stepping out from the Liberty Tree. "Two. Three . . ."

At eight paces, he was at the edge of the woods. After that it was more difficult to measure, as he could not continue in a straight line. But he dodged trees and brambles, keeping his eye on the track and estimating the distance as best he could. At what he guessed to be fourteen paces, he found himself in a cluster of boulders at the base of a large tree, with thick underbrush everywhere.

He frowned, looking for any sign of a silver box or white bit of paper. Could the next clue be up among the branches of the tree as the two others had been, or perhaps buried, like the one beneath that rosebush in Dorchester?

The light was fading fast, and he knew he should find a place to spend the night and come back in the morning. But now that he was so close, he couldn't bear to wait. Bending down, he did his best to push away the worst of the underbrush without getting pricked by the numerous thorns.

And then saw it. "A cave," he murmured in amazement, squinting to be certain he wasn't being tricked by a shadow.

Indeed, the boulders and underbrush hid a deep, narrow fissure in the earth. Crawling forward, now not caring or even noticing that the brambles tore at his clothes and skin, John felt around inside for a snuffbox or something of similar shape. Instead, his hand struck something much larger and more solid—a wooden trunk. When he pulled it out, with much sweating and swearing due to its immense weight, he found that it was filled with . . .

"Gunpowder!" he whispered, letting the gritty black substance run through his hands. For a moment he didn't understand. Was there another clue hidden somewhere in the powder? Feeling around inside the cave again, he soon realized it was crammed full of similar trunks. He pulled out one more and discovered that it contained muskets, pistols, bullet molds, powder horns, and other weaponry.

Now he understood. This was not another clue. It was the treasure!

"'*The treasure we shall require for right to triumph*'," he quoted aloud, remembering the note he had carried to Mr. Alden. For a moment he felt a twinge of disappointment. This was not a treasure like those he'd heard about as a child at his father's knee. No riches of the ancients. No Lost City of Gold.

Then he smiled. No, this treasure was much more important. An enormous secret cache of valuable munitions to help the Patriots should their quest for independence lead to war against the powerful and well-armed British regulars. Treasure indeed!

He closed both trunks and pushed them back into their hiding spot with the others. Then he carefully replaced the brush he'd moved aside, doing his best to make the spot look just as it had when he'd arrived. There were people who needed to know about this! It could mean the difference between success and failure of the colonies.

The next morning he set out toward Braintree, riding slowly to save his sluggish mount's energy and thinking hard all the while about what to do. Naturally, there was no way he could haul all those chests to Boston or Concord himself. With all the regulars on the roads these days, that wouldn't be safe anyway. Should he stop in Boston on his way home and contact Mr. Revere about the treasure? Or would it be better to alert George so that he and his fellow militiamen could retrieve it? Or perhaps he should have sought out the militia in Plymouth before leaving?

His head spun with possibilities. All along, finding the treasure had seemed the end of the quest. But now it seemed things had only grown more complicated.

Despite the inadequacies of his current horse, he reached Braintree around sunset. "Farewell, my lazy friend," he said, giving the beast one last pat as the stable boy led it away.

He stopped off to check on his mare, who seemed rested and content. Then he went into the inn, ready for a good night's rest himself. Maybe in the morning he would know what to do.

After his evening meal, he couldn't resist going out to the stable to check on Liberty again. While eating he had nearly settled on the idea of stopping in Boston to solicit Mr. Revere's advice, and he wanted to be sure she was fit and ready for the next day's ride.

By the time he had satisfied himself that all four of her legs were cool and tight and her breathing relaxed and regular, the moon had risen. He stopped outside, taking in gulps of the crisp, cool night air.

Just then he heard the sound of hooves galloping along the road. Stepping out to take a look, curious about who would be riding along so fast after dark, he saw a figure hunched aboard a plump roan horse. A strangely familiar roan horse, in fact . . .

"Help!" the rider shouted hoarsely, causing several doors and windows to open in the inn and nearby houses. "Someone, please—where is the inn?"

John gasped, recognizing Duncan's voice immediately. He stepped out and waved him down. "Duncan!" he cried. "What are you doing here?"

"Looking for you!" Duncan collapsed against his mount's neck, gulping in loud, ragged breaths. "Oh, John, thank God I have found you—I have already been to the inn at Weymouth and you were not there. I rode all the way from Concord today!"

"I can see that." John took the bridle and stared at Salem—for it was he—with concern. The big roan wasn't accustomed to such hard riding and was sweating and trembling with the exertion. "But what is of such urgent concern?"

Duncan slid down from the saddle, nearly collapsing as he landed on his good leg and it wobbled alarmingly. John caught him just in time.

"Easy, now," he said. "Why don't you wait and tell me in a moment when you've rested."

"It cannot wait," Duncan gasped out. "It is your father, John."

John's whole body went cold. Nearby, he was vaguely aware that the stable boy had arrived and was leading poor, exhausted Salem away, but he paid them no attention. He stared into Duncan's face. "What has happened to my father, Duncan?"

Duncan drew in a deep, shuddering breath. "Mr. Sims is accusing him of treason," he said. "And his charge is being backed by the odious Frederick of all people." His dark eyes bored into John's own. "If you don't do something, your father will be hanged at dawn tomorrow!"

Nineteen

John barely took the time to tighten Liberty's girth before swinging into the saddle. The mare danced nervously, clearly picking up on her rider's tense mood.

"But it is night," the stable boy exclaimed, seeming confused as he watched. "It is far too dangerous to ride out now!"

John ignored him, glancing at Duncan. "Thank you for coming for me," he told him. "Now stay here and rest. I'll take care of this."

"Be careful, John," Duncan pleaded.

John nodded. "Come, Liberty," he said, picking up the reins. "I shall need every ounce of your heart tonight."

He nudged the mare with his heels, and she responded eagerly, breaking at once into a high-stepping trot. Riding out onto the road, John turned one last time to wave good-bye to Duncan. Then he turned Liberty toward Concord and gave her her head.

"Let's go, girl!" he cried as she burst into a forward canter.

It was a long, harrowing ride through the moonlit Massachusetts countryside. John rode as fast as his horse could manage, dropping to a walk only when absolutely necessary. He also took every opportunity to leave the road for shortcuts through field and forest, thankful that he was riding his own brave, sure-footed mare, for no other horse could have made such a journey. The staccato beat of her hooves lent rhythm to the confused thoughts swirling about in his mind. Would he arrive in time? Even if he did, would he be able to stop what was about to happen? He did not know. He only knew he had to try.

They were splashing through a stream when the image of his father, smiling and dangling his feet off the bridge over the river as he explained some tricky code to a much younger John, floated across his mind. Hunching down over Liberty's withers, he urged her forward again, sending her from trot to gallop. The mare shook her head, but obeyed. Her dark coat was slick with sweat, but her legs ate up the miles, never faltering.

The first rays of the sun were creeping upward into the

sky when they finally reached the familiar countryside just outside of Concord. By then, both horse and rider were exhausted. But John urged Liberty from trot to canter once more, heading straight toward the village square.

By the time he got there, he found a crowd already gathered in front of the church. His father, flanked by Sims and another townsman, stood facing the group, his back ramrod straight and his expression defiant. Elizabeth, Alice, and the twins were weeping, huddled behind Oliver and Mary.

"Stop!" John shouted, leaping down from the saddle without a thought for his own fatigue. "You cannot do this!"

"John!" Alice cried. "Thank God you're here! You have to tell these people they're making a big mistake."

"There is no mistake," Sims retorted. "How can we trust a man who lets his own daughter consort with the regulars?"

Another man stepped forward, and John saw that it was Duncan's father. Mr. Winslow looked much like his son, except that both his legs were fully functional and instead of Duncan's open, eager, curious expression, the elder Winslow's face generally wore a look of sour suspicion.

"Indeed," Mr. Winslow spoke up. "Why, that Frederick

lout told me with a sneer that he and Alice were planning to wed and move back to England as soon as possible—and that Thomas Gates begged to come with them!"

John's eyes grew wider. Mr. Winslow's words were not that of a neutral. Had all of Concord gone mad while he was in Plymouth? He was about to say so when his father spoke up for the first time since John had arrived.

"Winslow, you are a liar," Thomas said evenly. "I said no such thing, and Alice has no such intentions."

"Father is right," Alice said with a sob. "Oh, I cannot believe this is happening!"

There were some murmurings from the watching crowd. John's heart pounded as he looked from one unfriendly, suspicious face to another. These were his neighbors. How could this be happening?

"It is not what you think," he said. "My father is as much a Patriot as any of us."

"That is what I've been telling them!" George called out, sounding angry. "But Sims and his friends refuse to listen. They are nearly as thickheaded as lobsterbacks themselves!"

"What? I'll not have you speak to me that way, boy!" Sims roared in fury, taking a step toward George.

George stepped forward as well, his expression grim. He towered over the older man by at least half a foot. "Are you going to stop me, sir?"

"Quit it!" Mary cried, hurrying forward and pushing George back. "All of you! Can't you see that we should all be on the same side?"

Meanwhile, Mr. Winslow was peering at John with a frown. "Where is my son?" he demanded. "You haven't dragged him off into trouble again, have you?"

"Duncan is fine." John turned away from him. "Now please, everyone, listen to me. If you are looking for traitors, you shall not find them in the Gates family. My father has been doing his part for the cause all along, supporting the Minutemen in all the ways he could." He pointed toward Alice. "As for my sister, she has been spending time with the regulars, yes. But only so she can learn their secrets."

Several young men had just arrived on the scene, looking rather confused. John recognized them from the times he'd watched George's Minuteman training—they were members of his militia.

Now one of them, a tough-looking man in his mid-twenties, stepped forward. "That is true, what he just told you," he said. "As an officer of the Concord militia, I can assure you that Miss Alice Gates has been bringing us information for some weeks now."

"Yes," said one of the other newcomers. "Now what is going on here?"

"They are accusing my father of treason," John spoke up.

"Your father?" the first officer said. "But aren't you John Gates? Why, Thomas Gates is the last person in Concord who should be accused of such things!"

By now the tenor of the crowd's murmurings had begun to change. As the other militia members spoke up, all of them vouching for Thomas with equal vehemence, John realized that the Minuteman from Lexington must not have been the only militiaman who had received free harnesswork from his father's shop.

"Thank you, boys," Thomas said to them. Then, once again glancing at his accusers, his expression darkened. "Dare you to hold me despite the testimony of these Minutemen, who are sworn to protect us all from our common threat?"

There were audible cries of "No, of course not!" and

"Our apologies, Gates" from throughout the crowd. Sims muttered something under his breath, then shrugged.

"I suppose it was a misunderstanding," he said at last. "I should not be so surprised that the lobsterback lied to us."

John's shoulders slumped with relief. He watched, too tired to move, as his father's captors stepped back and his sisters raced forward to fling themselves at him. It wasn't until Liberty nudged him in the back that he realized he was nearly asleep on his feet.

He was just leading the mare over to a nearby trough for a drink when Mr. Winslow caught up to him. "I still want an answer to my question, boy," the man growled. "Where is my son?"

"He should be back soon," John said wearily. "He is riding home from Braintree today."

"What? Braintree?" Winslow looked outraged. "What in the world is he doing there? And how dare you continue to influence him to defy my orders and sneak off hither and yon? Do not deny it, boy. I know you and that Chase boy are behind Duncan's recent disobediences."

That reminded John. He still needed to alert someone

as to what he'd found in Plymouth. At the moment, he felt
so exhausted that he wasn't sure he could stay upright long
enough to seek out the militia leaders and explain it all to
them. Nor did he have any energy left to fight with Mr.
Winslow.

"We have been seeking a treasure," he told Duncan's
father as Liberty dunked her nose into the trough and drank
deeply. "It all began when Mr. Paul Revere came to me one
day last summer—"

Mr. Winslow's small, dark eyes flashed with interest.

"He sent me to pick up a delivery from a friend of his
in Connecticut. . . ."

John went on to tell him the whole story, leaving out
the details of the clues but describing the way he, Duncan, and
George had tracked down the treasure all over Massachusetts
Colony—and how he had, less than two days ago, uncovered
the valuable munitions in the woods near Plymouth.

". . . and so now I need to let the Massachusetts militia
know of this cache," he finished. "Perhaps you could tell
them for me, sir? For I have been riding for the past
twenty-four hours almost without rest, and can think of
nothing at the moment but sleep."

242

"Of course, of course!" Winslow patted him on the arm. "I only wish you boys had confided in me about all this earlier; I might have been able to help. But do not worry, son—I shall take care of everything now."

"Thank you." Duncan's father was probably the last man in Concord they would have confided in, at least aside from an actual Tory! But it seemed the political climate was changing many things. He watched as the man hurried off toward the militiamen. At that moment, he saw George striding toward him.

"You arrived just in time, my friend," George said. "I was having no luck getting through to crazy Sims and his cronies. Now, did you have luck in Plymouth?"

"I did." John gave him the quick version of the story. "I shall give you all the details later," he continued. "I rode all night to get here, and am dead tired."

"Say no more." George reached for Liberty's bridle. "Here, I'll take care of your mare. Go home and get some rest." He glanced around at the townspeople, most of whom were now laughing and gossiping as if nothing had happened. "Everything will be all right now."

✳ ✳ ✳

John slept through the day, awakening only at dusk, feeling much refreshed. Hearing voices in the kitchen, he went in to find Duncan and Alice sitting close together. He smiled, relieved to see that his friend had made it home safely.

"Duncan!" he said, hurrying over. "Thanks again for—what's the matter?"

When Duncan had turned toward him, his face was grim. "My father, that's what's the matter!" Duncan exclaimed.

"Duncan . . ." Alice put a soothing hand on his arm, but Duncan shook it off, grabbed his cane, and stepped toward John.

"You told my father you found the treasure, yes?" Duncan said.

For a second, John wondered if Duncan was upset that he hadn't told him of his discovery in Braintree. He shrugged. "Yes, but . . ."

"Well, he has taken credit for the discovery himself!" Duncan exclaimed hotly. "Can you believe it? I never thought my own father would do such a thing!"

Seeing that John still looked confused, Alice spoke up.

"It seems that Mr. Winslow has told the militia that he found those munitions himself," she said. "As I have been telling Duncan, it is no surprise, really. There is neither honor nor safety in being known as neutral in these parts anymore. And what better way to curry favor with the Patriots than this?"

John's heart sank as he remembered that strange gleam in Winslow's eyes earlier. What better way indeed?

Before he could respond, his father strode into the kitchen. "John. There you are," Thomas said. "I wish to have a word with you."

"Come, Duncan." Alice rose and took Duncan's arm. "I'll walk you home if you like."

Soon John and his father were alone. "What's this I hear about a treasure?" Thomas asked gruffly. "I know that weaselly Winslow didn't really find it himself. Do you know anything of it, son?"

John gulped. "I thought of telling you, Father," he said. "It was just—there were so many clues, and we really didn't know what we were actually seeking, and in fact it's not exactly the ordinary type of treasure at all . . ." With that he was off, the words tumbling over one another in his haste.

He didn't quite dare meet his father's gaze as he told him the entire story. When he finally finished and looked up, he was surprised to see that Thomas was smiling.

"That's my boy," Thomas said, clapping him on the shoulder. "Those seem to have been some challenging clues. I taught you well, eh?"

John grinned, relieved. "Yes, I suppose you did, at that." Then his smile faded. "But Duncan just told me his father is claiming the find as his own. We have to tell everyone the truth—I can't stand the thought of Mr. Winslow taking the credit, especially after he accused you of treason based only on the word of the infernal Frederick!" He shrugged. "Besides, if the truth of the discovery becomes public it can only serve to improve our family name."

"Never mind Winslow." Thomas shrugged. "He is weak of will and does not matter. Neither does it matter what anyone says of the Gates family. Haven't I told you that before?"

"You have." John frowned, not fully satisfied. "But I still think it is important that people know the truth."

"The only matter of importance is that the treasure was found," Thomas said. "Now if the worst should happen and those munitions prove to be needed, they will be available to help the cause of justice. Of course, we all hope it shall not actually come to that. . . ."

John just nodded, deciding he had to think more on the matter to figure out what to make of all that had happened in the past few days. In the meantime, even his long sleep had not fully chased the weariness from his mind and body.

"I think I shall have a quick bite of food and then return to bed," he told Thomas, stifling a yawn. "It has been a hard few days."

Thomas dropped a hand on John's shoulder again and this time left it there a moment. "All right, son," he said. "I shall see you in the morning."

A short while later John was back in bed. But tired as he was, his mind was too active to allow sleep to overtake him. He lay there for several hours, tossing and turning and thinking of all that had happened.

He was finally dozing off sometime after midnight when a sudden clatter of hooves in the street just outside roused him again. Then there came a shout:

"The regulars are coming out! The regulars are coming out!"

"What?" John murmured. Hopping out of bed, he

peered out the window to see a rider on a dark horse gallop past. He quickly pulled on his shirt and breeches and headed for the door, ignoring the confused calls of his sisters as they began to awaken as well.

He burst out onto the street to find the horseman circling back, still shouting out his message. Farther up the street, sleepy voices were beginning to be heard as others awoke. John stepped out and hailed the rider.

"Who are you, and what is it you are saying, sir?" he called.

"It is the regulars, lad!" the rider replied, reining his lathered horse to a halt. "My name is Prescott—Dr. Samuel Prescott. I was riding through Lexington and encountered two men, a Mr. William Dawes and a Mr. Paul Revere. They were spreading the word—the regulars plan to attack at dawn! They are after the weapons stores here at Concord!"

John gasped. Could it be true? Was this the attack on the munitions supplies that had been rumored for weeks? His heart pounded.

Prescott spurred his horse onward, again taking up his cry: "The regulars are coming! The regulars are coming out!"

He rode off down the road toward the center of town.

Meanwhile John turned back into his house, hurrying to find his boots and coat and wake his father. If the regulars were indeed coming to attack Concord this April morn, he was ready to do whatever he could to protect it. He had worked so hard and sacrificed so much already for the cause of freedom—he was not about to stop now.

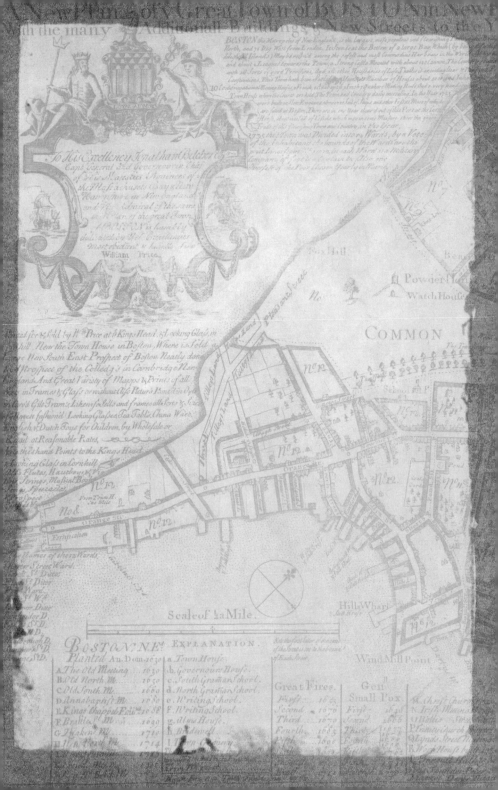

Post Script

Like the films *National Treasure* and *National Treasure: Book of Secrets* that inspired it, this is a fictional story grounded in real facts and history. John Raleigh Gates, his family and two best friends, and some of the other characters are invented, but many others who appear in the story were real people who lived at that time, and many of the events that John witnesses actually did take place in the year and a half leading up to the American Revolutionary War.

During those years, much of the populace of the thirteen colonies was indeed divided into Patriots—those who wanted independence from England—and Loyalists, who as the name indicates, remained loyal to the British king. There were also those who remained neutral in the conflict.

Among the famous Patriots in and around Boston at that time were Paul Revere, Samuel Adams, and John Hancock, all of them members of the Sons of Liberty.

Paul Revere is famous for his "midnight ride," as mentioned

near the end of the story, but even before that he did his part for the Patriot cause, acting as a messenger for Boston's Committee of Public Safety and also creating political engravings. He had a silversmith's shop at Dock-Square in Boston during this period, and his house still stands today as a historical monument.

Samuel Adams is probably best known today for the beer that bears his name, but at the time of the American Revolution he was a leader of the resistance movement in Boston and the surrounding area. He was very active in politics, being one of the first to champion the idea of independence from England. He took part in protests against the Stamp Act of 1765 and did indeed speak at the meeting immediately before the Boston Tea Party. He took part in the First Continental Congress in Philadelphia as well as the Second Continental Congress, where he was one of the signers of the Declaration of Independence.

Speaking of the Declaration of Independence, most people know that John Hancock was the first person to sign that document. He was also a political agitator, the first governor of Massachusetts, and at one time the wealthiest man in New England. Like Paul Revere, George Washington, Benjamin Franklin, and many other well-known historical figures, he was a Freemason.

Other real-life figures who appear in the story are:

*Nathan Hale, who really did believe in, and provide, education for girls and was a member of Yale's Linonian Society, but who is remembered today for the famous quote "I only regret that I have but one life to give for my country," which he was reported to have said just before being hanged by the British at age twenty-one.

*Justin Morgan, a music teacher and horse breeder, whose stallion, Figure, was the foundation of the Morgan horse breed.

*Samuel Osgood, who was the first postmaster general of the U.S. (His cousin Charles was created for this book, however, as was his meeting with Revere, Adams, and Hancock.)

Several other historical figures are mentioned as well, though they do not actually appear. Benjamin Franklin did in fact create the political cartoon "Join, or Die" during the French and Indian War. George Washington really did have a favored chestnut horse named Nelson, along with another horse known as Blueskin who was probably gray. Infamous turncoat Benedict Arnold may never have spent an evening drinking with Paul

Revere, but he did create a book cipher (the Arnold Cipher) with which he communicated with his coconspirator. Charles Carroll, a signer of the Declaration of Independence, really did once write a series of newspaper articles under the pseudonym "First Citizen." (He also appears in the flashback scene near the beginning of *National Treasure*.) General Gage and Governor Hutchinson were real people, too. So were Patrick Henry, George Mason, William Blaxton, Isaac Barré, Crispus Attucks, and Pope Clement XIV.

Real-life events seen or mentioned in this book include the Boston Tea Party (known in that time as "the Destruction of the Tea" and featuring the ships the *Dartmouth*, the *Eleanor*, and the *Beaver*), the Powder Alarm, the First Continental Congress (known in its day, of course, only as "the Continental Congress"), the Hutchinson Letters Affair, and the Boston Massacre (including the real initials of the five victims). Then, of course, there were the Battles of Lexington and Concord, which John Gates is about to take part in at the end of this book. These skirmishes took place on April 19, 1775, and are considered the first military engagements of the Revolutionary War—and have been referred to as "the shot heard 'round the world."

Real-life documents mentioned include the Fairfax Resolves, the Stamp Act and the Stamp Act Congress, the Intolerable Acts (which included the Quartering Act), the Mayflower Compact, the Suffolk Resolves, and *The True Sentiments of America*, which included writings by Samuel Adams.

Real-life locations include all the towns mentioned as well as specific sites including Faneuil Hall (with its copper grasshopper weathervane), the Boston Liberty Tree, Copp's Hill Burial Ground, and the Old North Church, of "one if by land, two if by sea" fame.

In addition, the Minutemen (part of the Massachusetts Militia) were real. Dartmouth College really was founded in 1769 as a school for educating the native Indian population. Davison, Newman, and Co. was the name of the company whose tea was destroyed in the Boston Tea Party. And the Liberty Bell (which remains on display to this day in Philadelphia) was then known as the Independence Bell or the Old State House Bell and contains the verse quoted in this story as part of its inscription.

And finally, John's job as a post rider was a real occupation in colonial times. In those days, long before e-mail, faxes, or even the telephone, letters were the primary means of communication between people separated by any distance. However, there was no real organized national postal service until after the revolution. Before that time, letters might be carried by friends, traveling merchants, or the hired horsemen known as post riders (some of whom, unlike John, traveled along regular routes between towns or cities). It took a long time to travel by horseback, and on long journeys a rider would stop to spend his nights at the closest tavern or inn (it was dangerous to ride at night due to wild animals, lack of light, and other hazards). If necessary, he could also trade his horse in for a fresher mount at the local livery stable, which kept horses for that purpose.

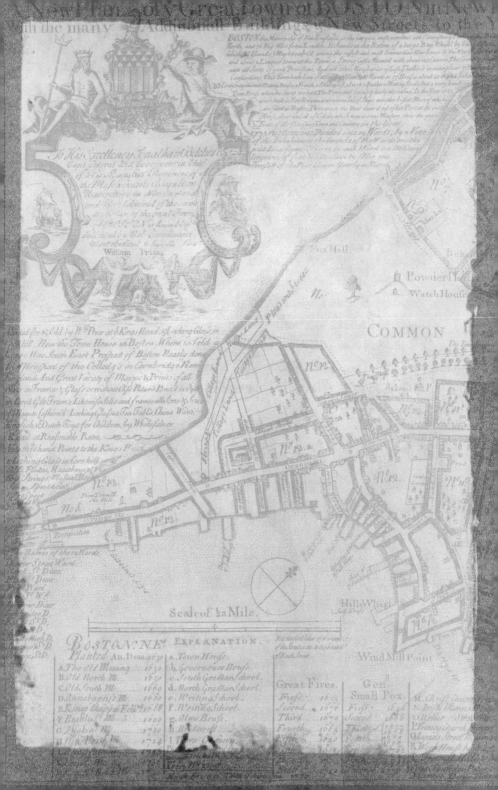

DON'T MISS THE NEXT VOLUME...

UNCHARTED

℀ A GATES *Family Mystery* ℀

The Revolutionary War has been won. The United States of America is now struggling to broaden her boundaries. And as new territories are claimed and named, two siblings discover the high price of freedom.

Adam Benjamin Gates and his twin sister, Eleanor, have heard their father's tales of his part in the Revolutionary War and his discovery of a great treasure that helped the Patriots. But they long for an adventure of their own. So when they hear whispers of a voyage to explore the recently purchased Louisiana territory, the siblings are determined to take part. Soon, Adam and Eleanor find themselves on a dangerous journey into uncharted lands. But the greatest danger is yet to come, when they learn of a treasure hidden deep in the wilderness.

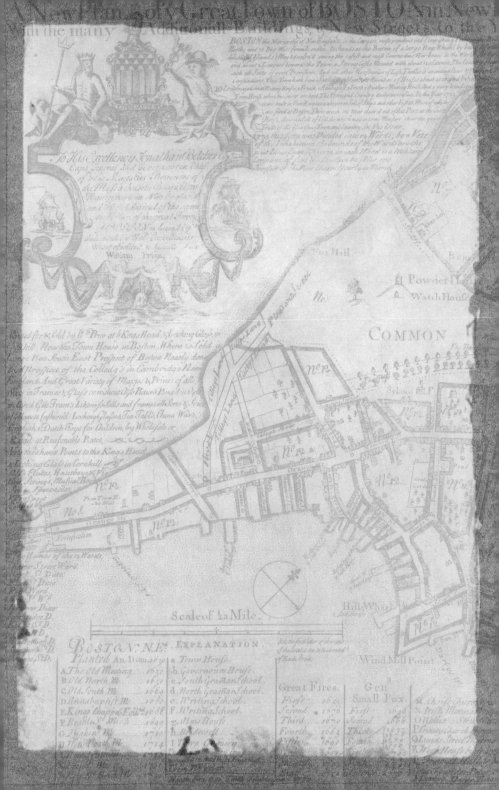

Charles River

Ferry to Charles-Town
several happening

E. N. Mill Dam

Mills Pond

No 1

No 4

No 6

No 9

No 9

No 9

Old Wharf

Old Wharf

Old Wharf

Fort Hill
No 10

S. Battery.

HARBOUR